GUNMAN'S PEACE

....

MILTON J DAVIS

MVmedia, LLC
Fayetteville, Georgia

MVmedia, LLC
PO Box 1465
Fayetteville, GA 30214
www.mvmediaatl.com

Publisher's Note: This is a work of fiction. Names, characters, places, and incidents are a product of the author's imagination. Locales and public names are sometimes used for atmospheric purposes. Any resemblance to actual people, living or dead, or to businesses, companies, events, institutions, or locales is completely coincidental.

Book Layout ©2017 BookDesignTemplates.com
Cover Art by Edison Moody
Interior Art by Quinn McGowan
Cover Design by Kecia Stovall

Ordering Information:
Quantity sales. Special discounts are available on quantity purchases by corporations, associations, and others. For details, contact the "Special Sales Department" at the address above.

Gunman's Peace/Milton J Davis. -- 1st ed.
ISBN 978-0-9992789-8-7

Contents

To A Better Future

Moses Pritchard sat cross-legged in the tree stand overlooking Crim Valley, rubbing his beard as he watched the village below. For three days he observed the villagers go about their daily routine and he was getting aggravated. This was Retriever work. But orders were orders, so he calmed down and waited for further instructions.

"Moses?"

He tapped the object in his ear, answering his comm.

"Yeah, go ahead."

"Sanchez spotted a truck convoy heading in your direction two days ago," the voice on the other end said.

"Slavers?"

"Don't know. There were no armored cars, just trucks. They seemed to be travelling light, moving fast."

"Coming from the south?"

"Like always."

Moses lowered his binoculars then leaned against the long-leafed pine as he massaged his forehead.

"I'm tired of going in circles with these people. Just send in the damned Retrievers and bring them in already."

"You know the rules," the voice said. "Assimilation must be voluntary. Otherwise we're no better than slavers."

Moses spat.

"Yeah, yeah. If it was up to me, I'd drag their assess behind the Perimeter kicking and screaming. They'd thank me later."

"That's why it's not up to you."

The rumble of heavy vehicles stole Moses' attention. He lifted the binoculars, looking to the ragged highway snaking through the dense pines.

"The trucks are here," he commented.

"What do you see?"

The vehicles sped down the highway then veered onto the two-lane leading into the village. They continued into the central square, filling the roundabout before stopping and blocking traffic. Christopher Tolbert, the village elder, emerged from the elders' compound covered in his rank robe, his gray beaded braids bouncing off his narrow shoulders. He strolled to the trucks, his hands opened in the traditional village greeting. Armed men leapt from the truck. One of them leveled his AR-15 at Christopher then emptied his clip into the man's chest.

"Slavers!" Moses shouted. He clambered down the tree then sprinted to his bike.

"Back up is on the way," the voice said. "Hold your position until they arrive."

"Not enough time," Moses said. "I'm going in."

"Moses wait! You can't . . ."

Moses chambered rounds in his 9mm Sig Sauer handguns then started the bike.

"Yes I can. I'm a Neutralizer, remember?"

Moses sped down the narrow trail then merged onto the main highway. In minutes he was at the town's outskirts, streaking by villagers fleeing the intruders. With his left hand he pulled out the handgun from the hostler nestled under his right arm, blasting two slavers chasing the villagers. He downed two more slavers on his way to the town center. Fiver slavers lay dead by the time he jumped from the bike. The bike crashed into the rear of the truck then both vehicles caught fire. Moses scrambled to his feet then ran for cover. Minutes later the truck exploded, killing those slavers too foolish to seek cover.

"Moses?" the voice said. "Are you okay? What's going on?"

Moses weaved through the remaining trucks, exchanging gunfire with the slavers as bullets whizzed by his head.

"I'm in town center," he shouted as he ducked between two battered trucks. "Five slavers are down, about ten wounded. I figure ten, maybe fifteen still standing but not for long."

"Moses, disengage!" the voice commanded. "Our team is almost there!"

A slaver jumped around the truck facing Moses, an automatic pressed into his gut. Moses sidestepped as the man fired then shot him in the chest, blowing him from behind the truck.

"Moses! Get out of there now!"

"Shut the fuck up!" Moses said. He shut off his head set.

He was taking fire from all sides, pinned between the trucks.

"Divide and conquer, homeboy," he whispered. He took out his second magnum.

"Let's do this!"

Moses sprinted to his right, guns in both hands. Three slavers stepped out to cut him off and Moses shot them down, one shot for each man. Before the other slavers could pursue, he disappeared behind the nearest building. He holstered his magnums then took his HK MP5 from his back.

"Time to go hunting," he said. He worked his way between the buildings and vehicles, hunting down the slavers with methodical precision. One shot, one man. The last slaver cowered behind a small jeep, his head exposed. Moses raised the HK then took aim. The man seemed to sense his predicament; he stood, his shaking hands raised over his head.

"I give up! I give up!"

Moses's finger tightened on his trigger.

"It's a little late for that," he said.

"Moses, no!"

Moses hesitated. He turned then stared into the eyes of Amanda Berkowitz. Her dirty gray hair fell off her head in disarray, blood splattered on her blouse, apron and skirt. She pressed her small hands against her chest, the village posture for prayer.

"Come on Amanda, don't do this," Moses said. "You let this bastard go and he'll be back with friends."

"I won't! I swear to God I won't!" the man said. Tears escaped his wide brown eyes.

"We've had enough of your brand of salvation today Moses Pritchard," Amanda said. "Let him go."

Moses lowered his gun. "I don't understand you people," he muttered.

He walked to the man, his gun still trained on him. When he reached him, he smashed the gunstock against the slaver's head. The man fell to all fours as he moaned.

"Get the fuck out of here," Moses said. "If you're smart you won't come back."

The man scrambled to his feet then ran for the lead truck, the only one untouched by Moses' attack. Moses raised his gun, firing off a round that struck the ground before the man's right foot.

"No, buddy. You're walking out of here."

The man sprinted by the truck, through the other burning vehicles then down the main road.

Moses slung HK across his back then glared at Amanda.

"You'll be seeing him again," he said.

"Maybe not," Amanda replied. Villagers emerged from their hiding places to care for the wounded and collect the dead. Amanda trudged to the crowd that surrounded Christopher's body. Together they prayed, their voices barely louder than a whisper. When they were done Amanda stepped away.

"Let's get him buried," she said. "No use staring any longer. Chris is gone to Glory."

Moses lost his temper.

"When are you people going to listen to reason?" he shouted. "As long as you stay Outside this is going to happen. You'll all be gone to Glory before the year's out!"

"Mr. Pritchard!" Amanda strode him, standing so close their noses almost touched.

"I will not let you use this tragedy to further Newlanta's agenda! It's not your place to do so!"

"You're correct Amanda. It's not his place. It's mine."

Thomas Dern stepped between Moses and Amanda, his wide white smile in contrast to his umber skin. He wore his usual khakis and laced boots, although the uniform looked more like a casual outfit on him than a soldier's uniform. Moses had been so distracted he didn't hear the Retrievers arrive.

Thomas was a tall, attractive man, the perfect eye candy for retrieval duty. He shared a sympathetic smile with Amanda as he took her hand.

"My team will tend to the burials and your wounded," he said.

"We can take care of our own," Amanda replied, the harshness gone from her voice.

"I know, but we wish to help," Thomas said. "It's the least we can do."

Amanda kissed Thomas's cheek. "Thank you, Thomas. God bless you."

She scowled at Moses before walking away.

Thomas held onto his smile until Amanda was gone from view before snapping his head around to face Moses.

"God damn it Moses! What were you trying to do?"

Moses shrugged then folded his arms. "Look around you. I didn't 'try' to do anything. You've been trying to sweet talk these assholes into Newlanta for three years. Thought I'd try some tough love. I'm tired of saving people that don't want to be saved."

"It's your job," Thomas retorted. "If you have a problem, complain to Voorhees . . . or leave."

"Maybe I'll do both," Moses said. He sauntered to one of the dead slavers, knelt beside him then searched his pockets until he found keys. He climbed into the closest truck, inserted the key into the ignition then twisted it. The truck coughed then rumbled to life.

"What are you doing?" Thomas asked.

"I blew up my bike, so I'm taking the truck," Moses said.

"The trucks belong to the village now," Thomas said.

"Not this one. I'll see you back at the ranch."

"I'm filing a report!" Thomas yelled.

"Can't wait to read it." Moses backed up the truck then steered it around.

"See you later, Tommy Boy!"

Thomas's shook a fist at Moses as he drove away.

"I told you not to call me that!"

Teasing Thomas pulled Moses out of his sour mood. He maneuvered the truck through the debris strewn street, following the two-lane highway to I-75 North. He paused for a moment, checking in both directions to make sure there were no other slavers waiting to rendezvous with the team he neutralized before he exited on to the highway toward Newlanta. As he headed north, he took in the sights along the highway. The world was healing. What people had not been able to reclaim nature filled in, giving the hilly landscape a hopeful look. Not too long ago the stretch of road he was driving was a death trap; now a person could travel in reasonable safety, thanks to Newlanta. His mind flashed back to his days in the Wild, hiding with papa and mama, scratching a life out of the ruins and wreckage of the Collapse. The world was waking up even then though he couldn't see it through his young eyes. Sometimes they would venture near Newlanta, its imposing Perimeter wall rising over the surrounding ruins and stunted pines. Back then it was a place no one wanted to enter. Now it was a symbol of hope for a peaceful future.

The forests gave way to small settlements as he neared the city. This was another change, something that would never have existed twenty years ago. People felt bold enough to gather in communities and set down permanent roots, at least under the watchful eye of the Perimeter towers. There were other settlements scattered throughout the Georgia territory, but they were ruled by warlords and the inhabitants were more captives than citizens. Moses coughed as he recalled his part in the subjugation of many of those folks. Those were the days he worked as a hired gun, earning a reputation as a man valued as an ally and feared as an enemy.

The Perimeter Wall appeared over the next hill and Moses smiled. This was home now, at least for the foreseeable future. It was ironic that a wall built to imprison the city's inhabitants was now a barrier to protect those same citizens from the surrounding chaos. No one was sure who built the it; some say the Feds constructed it to protect its interests before the Collapse; others say the Conservatives raised it to separate themselves from Liberal forces that had gathered in the city during the height of the violence. Whatever the reasons, the result was a self-contained prosperous community dedicated to the creation of a peaceful, sustainable society.

Although Newlanta was generous about spreading its influence beyond its walls, it was protective when it came to letting influences in. Moses drove the confiscated truck to the South Gate, stopping just short of the guard posts. He fished through his coat pockets for his papers as the armed guard approached his window. The guard smiled as Moses rolled down the window.

"Hey Moses," the guard said.

"What's up, Taylor?"

"Same old shit. New ride?"

"Broke my bike," Moses replied as he handed Taylor his entry papers. Though he was well known Voorhees and the elders were sticklers for protocol.

"The motor pool will be happy to hear that."

The guard looked over his papers then handed them back.

"Oh, I'm supposed to tell all Neutralizers that there will be a meeting at headquarters first thing tomorrow morning."

"Shit. I wasn't planning on staying Outside tonight," Moses said.

"You got no choice, killer," the guard said, using the Neutralizer nickname.

Moses studied Taylor with fresh eyes.

"You a Neutralizer?"

"Used to be," the guard replied.

Moses pushed back into his seat. There was a time when he knew them all; now they were signing up and getting out too fast for him to track. The thought depressed him so he decided to change the subject.

"Where can I crash?"

"I heard it's tight. You might have to crash at HQ."

"Thanks, killer," Moses said. "Keep'em wide."

"Don't miss," the guard replied.

Moses steered the truck through the narrow gate then headed to the motor pool. He passed through a few communities on his way to the pool, each clustered around a communal farm that sustained them. The Piedmont Market dominated the city center, a multi-level market where communities traded goods on the ground level. The upper floors were reserved for planting and small livestock, a vertical farm rising over its patrons. The Market was surrounded by the skeletal remains of old towers swarming with workers reclaiming the metal and other items to be used in the communities. The absence of mega-corporations made such buildings obsolete. The world emerging from the ashes of the Collapse was a simpler world that eschewed rampant greed. At least that was the plan. Somebody would have to tell the warlords sooner or later.

Moses reached the motor pool, the squat building hidden behind the Newlanta Facilities Center. Enormous searchlights lit the cavernous pre-fab as he parked the vehicle, jumped out then scampered away as fast as he could.

"Where the hell is my goddamn bike?" a gruff voice demanded.

Moses dropped his chin.

"I broke it, Snake."

A large hand gripped his shoulder then spun him about. The wide bearded sun-burned face of Snake Dobarzinski greeted him.

"What do you think this is Prichard?"

Snake raised his filthy hands in Moses's face.

"Look at my hands. This is grease boy, not magic dust. I don't pull those bikes out my ass. I build them with these and it's damn hard work!"

"I'll try to remember that the next time I'm getting shot at," Moses replied.

"You Neutralizers think you can do whatever you want!" Snake shouted. "This is the last time you get a bike from me!"

"Enjoy the truck, Snake," Moses said as he tossed the mechanic the keys then strolled away. He was tired and Snake's whining was beginning to piss him off. He would hate to shoot Newlanta's best mechanic, but if he let that man's spittle splash his face one more second there was going to be a funeral.

Moses had no intentions of staying in the HQ barracks. He would head to Zenobia's and hope she would let him crash for a few days. As he sauntered toward the Peachtree Towers, he hoped Zenobia wasn't pissed at him, too. He just wanted to sleep and she was his only option.

He reached the Towers, one of the few high-rise structures not being cannibalized. It served as a home for new arrivals as they sought a community to join. Zenobia had lived there longer than most; like Zeke her skills were limited so few communities were eager to take her in. Until then she worked as a scavenger, her contribution for being allowed to live in the city. 'For every person a purpose,' the Newlanta saying went.

Moses entered the lobby then walked to the buzz plate. He hit the button to Zenobia's flat then waited.

"What, Carmen?" she slurred.

"Guess again."

There was a brief moment of silence before she spoke again.

"Moses? Is that you?"

"Yeah babe, it's me. Buzz me up."

"Okay, okay. Give me a minute to tidy up."

"You know I don't care about stuff like that," Moses said.

"I do," Zenobia replied. "Five minutes, okay?"

"Okay."

Moses was annoyed, but he didn't have a choice. He leaned against the wall, then picked at his fingernails until he heard the buzz. The elevator opened and he entered. The car zoomed up to the 23rd floor then the doors swished open. Moses strolled down the dimly lit hallway until he arrived at Zenobia's flat.

Moses knocked on the door. The peephole cover slid open.

"Cheese!" he said as he smiled.

The door swung open and Zenobia appeared, a wide smile on her smooth brown face.

"Hi baby!" he said.

Zenobia answered with a hug and all the tension flowed out of his body. He never realized how much he missed her until he was with her, holding her warm body against his.

Zenobia pressed her hand against his chest. She pecked his lips then frowned.

"You stink."

"I guess I need a bath."

"Yes you do. Come on."

She pulled him into the apartment and he took off his guns, holsters, body armor and uniform.

"You have credits?" she asked.

"Always."

Moses looked around the apartment.

"Where's Carmen?"

"She's at work."

"Damn. I was hoping you kicked her out so I could move in."

Zenobia stepped out of her room wearing a tight-fitting one piece.

"You never liked her," she said.

"I don't trust her. I told you she came at me a few times."

Zenobia sucked her teeth. "Whatever. The girl puts in her worktime. I don't know when you're going to leave or when you're coming back. Besides, it's only temporary. As soon as I get an okay from a community I'm gone."

"How's that going?"

"Still looking, but I'm hopeful."

Zenobia grabbed his hand then led him to the door.

"Come on. Let's get you cleaned up."

They took the elevator to Manny's Spa on the top floor. The spa was a rare luxury in the city, a respite for the hard-working volunteers, but it wasn't free. Manny's was one of the few places allowed to charge its patrons, but that was to end soon. It was a remnant of the old ways and the Elders were determined to rid itself of such practices.

The glare from the pulsing neon sign illuminated the dark corridor. A stout smiling woman with an alabaster complex and platinum blonde hair stood behind the podium at the entrance.

"Welcome to Manny's...oh, hey Zee!"

"Hey Christine. I'd like you to meet Moses."

Christine's eyes widened. "So, you're the famous Moses Pritchard. It's good to finally meet you. The way Zee's been talking about you I thought you'd have wings."

"Shut up, girl," Zenobia replied. "Is the Jacuzzi open?"

"For you it is," Christine replied

Moses dug into his pocket for credits but Christine shook her head.

"You're with my girl. Don't worry about it. Here's the access code." She handed Zenobia a paper card with the code printed on it.

Zenobia grasped Moses hand then led him through the workout area to the conditioning room at the rear of the spa. She punched in the combination code and the metal door slid aside. It was obvious the room was not set up for tired workers or athletes. Cool jazz hovered in the dim light, the eletro-candles flickering with the smooth rhythm. The Jacuzzi began to fill automatically, the gurgling water pushing the music into the background. The room's warmth made clothes uncomfortable; Zenobia and Moses watched each other undress with eager eyes. They stepped into the half-full tub. Moses closed his eyes and settled into the soothing, swirling liquid, spreading his long arms along the top of the Jacuzzi as he leaned back his head. Zenobia snuggled beside him, laying her head on his collarbone.

"It should be a crime to feel this good," he said.

Zenobia placed her palm on his chest, playing in the roughness of his curly black chest hairs.

"Was it bad?" she asked.

"It's always bad," he replied. "Slavers from the south this time. They killed a mayor and shot up a few villagers before I showed up."

"I don't see how you still do it," Zenobia said.

Moses stiffened. "I don't see how I couldn't."

Zenobia pulled away from him. "I wish you would quit. There's plenty of work to be done in the city. I know you got skills."

"You know I can't," he said.

"Can't or won't?"

Moses sat up then looked Zenobia in the eyes.

"Look baby, I'm tired. I know how this argument is going to end. Let's just call it a night. I can stay at the barracks."

Zenobia shook her head then hugged him. Moses wrapped his arms around her.

"I just don't want to lose you, that's all," she said.

"You won't."

"You can't promise me that. You're not bulletproof."

Moses looked into Zenobia's eyes again. She wanted him to quit for her. She wanted him to stop because she loved him. But he didn't love her. Whenever he came close the same image would appear, the vision of a child watching his mother then his father die. He learned long ago that the worst pain in the world was when you lost someone you loved. He vowed never to go through that again.

"I want to do it babe, but I can't handle it right now. I've got to be out there."

"I'm not going to win this argument, am I?"

Moses shook his head.

Zenobia draped her arms on his shoulders then wrapped her legs around his waist.

"I don't know where you'll be tomorrow, but I know where you are right now. I might as well make the best of it."

Moses and Zenobia cavorted in the hot tub until their skin wrinkled like raisins. They returned to the apartment, changed clothes, then went to the local market to pick up items for dinner. When they returned to the apartment Carmen was there.

"Look who's back!" Carmen said.

Moses managed a smile. "Hey Carmen."

"Don't get too excited," she said. "I'm not staying. I'll give you two love birds some space."

"You don't have to go," Zenobia said.

"Yes, I do. I'm not about to put up with all the noise y'all will be making tonight."

She hugged Zenobia, then kissed Moses's cheek. He winced.

"Glad to see you back from the Wild," she said.

"Yeah. Bye, Carmen."

Carmen left the apartment.

"I know you don't like her, but you didn't have to be rude," Zenobia said.

"Did you see what she did?" Moses said. "She kissed me on the cheek. In front of you!"

Zenobia waved her hand. "That's Carmen. She's all touchy feely. She doesn't mean anything by it. You're taking it the wrong way."

Zenobia carried the groceries to the sink.

"We're not going to argue about Carmen. She's gone. Come over here and help me make dinner."

Moses chopped the vegetables while Zenobia prepared the chicken. It felt good to do something that didn't involve taking a person's life. That was the reason he finally came to Newlanta, to put down his guns and live in peace. But it seemed like that was not his destiny. A few people inside recognized him and reported him to the Elders. They hoped he would be punished for what he was, but instead they recruited him.

They sat down to a quiet, intimate meal, the first fresh food Moses had in weeks. After the meal they spent the rest of the evening on the couch, cuddling and small talking. Zenobia was good to him and good for him, but he couldn't say that he was the same for her. He wanted to be, but there were things in his past that prevented him from getting too close.

That night after making love Moses couldn't sleep. He eased out of the bed and back into the kitchen area. He sat still, enjoying the quiet, enjoying the peace. He never got used to it, resting without having to be on guard. That's what Newlanta offered. That's why he agreed to pick up his guns again.

"Baby?"

Moses turned to see Zenobia standing at the door.

"You okay?" she asked.

"Yeah, baby. I'm fine."

"Come back to bed," she said.

Moses pushed back the chair then sauntered up to her. He picked up, and they kissed as he carried her back to bed.

- 2 -

The insistent beep of his alarm pulled Moses
out of his blissful slumber. He sat up then look to
his right. Zenobia lay naked beside him on her
stomach, her body rising and falling with her
breathing. He smiled as he ran his hand from her
neck to her finely shaped butt, giving it a gentle
squeeze. She shifted and sighed.
"That feels good," she said.
"It does," Moses replied. "But I have to go."
Zenobia rolled onto her back then reached
for him.
"Right now?"
Moses leaned over and kissed her, careful
not to get too close.
"Yeah. I got a meeting."
Zenobia sat up, wrapped her arms around
his neck then pulled him on top of her.
"Well, you're going to be late."
Moses buried his face into her neck.
"I guess I am."

* * *

The meeting began at eight sharp in the East Newlanta market on Ponce. The old structure existed long before the Collapse, morphing into various identities during its lifetime. Now it was headquarters of the Newlanta Reclamation Department or NRD, the department responsible for rebuilding the city and establishing safe districts surrounding the Perimeter Wall. It was also the department overseeing the Assimilation and Prevention Project, home of the Retrievers and Neutralizers. The meeting room was cavernous; the metal chairs in formation in the corner across from the entrance. Retrievers and Neutralizers segregated themselves, the straight-laced Retrievers taking the first row because of their aggressive punctuality. The Neutralizers lounged in the back, chatting and laughing.

Moses sauntered into the room. As he neared the back row a tall dark-skinned man dressed in the drab grey NRD uniform took the podium. The room fell silent as he scanned the group with penetrating brown eyes that focused on Moses as he took his seat.

"Eight oh one, Mister Pritchard," he said.

"Great," Moses said. "You can tell time."

Commander Darin Voorhees glared at Moses and Moses smiled back. A few of the Retrievers turned around to glare at Moses while the Neutralizers laughed and winked. Voorhees directed his attention to the group.

"A situation has occurred that requires the immediate attention of everyone in this room. We have reason to believe a particular southern warlord has acquired the means to jeopardize the safety of Newlanta."

The Retrievers murmured nervously. The words had the opposite effect on the Neutralizers. They all fell silent, including Moses. Voorhees let his words settle before continuing.

"The recent increase in slaver raids drew our attention further south. We contracted Uta Jones to do an aerial reconnaissance. Uta?"

Moses smirked as his old friend sauntered to the podium. Uta Jones was a head shorter than Voorhees and possessed the hard, lean body and suspicious eyes of a man from the Wild. He nodded to Voorhees before speaking.

"From the air the truck patterns are obvious," he said. "They lead to two convergence points, one about forty miles from the coast, the other ten miles sought of the 16/75 junction."

Uta looked at Moses as he mentioned the last location. Moses cut a glance at Voorhees, expecting the same expression. He wasn't disappointed.

Uta stepped aside as Voorhees returned to the podium.

"These are locations of former military installations Stewart and Robbins. It's possible whoever is doing this is planning a major military campaign, and we may be the target."

Darin returned to the podium.

"Because of this threat your orders have changed. Assimilation for settlement within a fifty-mile radius of Newlanta is mandatory. Retriever and Neutralizer teams will be combined into Persuader teams to encourage evacuations."

Thomas Dean stood. "This is against protocol, commander."

"There is no protocol when it comes to the survival of Newlanta," Voorhees replied.

"I wish to file a formal protest to the Elders!" Dean retorted.

"These orders come from them," Voorhees said. "But feel free to share your dissatisfaction."

Thomas scowled then sat.

Voorhees waited for more protests before continuing. There were none.

"I need the retrieval team commanders to coordinate their schedules with the Neutralizers. I expect to see new residents as soon as yesterday."

Voorhees left the podium; the meeting was over. Moses sauntered to him.

"You need to speak to me?"

Voorhees nodded. "Follow me."

Moses, Uta and Voorhees walked to the rear of the building to Voorhees's office. The office was at the end of a dim corridor which extended from the meeting hall. The room was bare and functional; a large metal desk with two chairs opposite his. The walls were bare. Voorhees sat behind his desk and rubbed his forehead. Uta and Moses sat in the chairs on the opposite side. Moses turned to Uta.

"So what's the deal?"

Uta pushed his chair back onto the rear legs.

"It's definitely a buildup. I'm seeing fires and raided communities up and down the coast and the highways. Somebody is building an involuntary labor force. I think Stewart is random, probably some local upstart. But Robbins is definitely organized. They're probably scavenging the military bases for ammo and weapons."

"Somebody we know?" Moses asked.

Uta frowned. "Most likely."

Moses turned to Voorhees. "What do you need me to do?"

"I need you to go to Robbins," he said.

"When do I leave?" Moses asked.

"As soon as this meeting is over. Find out which warlord is stirring up trouble and what they're up to."

A chill swept over Moses.

"Is Newlanta going to war?"

"It depends on what you find," Voorhees replied.

Moses folded his arms across his chest as his past flashed before him. He was twelve, an oiled AK-47 gripped in his callow hands as he followed his father through a thick stand of loblolly pines, the summer sun squeezing sweat out of him like a sour wash rag. He crouched low like his daddy taught him, staring into his broad back as they advanced on the heavy machine gun position in the clearing. The fear came on him like it was yesterday. Mama had been dead three years, her memory still sharp in his young mind. Their life had transformed after her passing. They'd become nomads, settling wherever an ambitious warlord needed skilled gunmen. He blinked his eyes and returned to the present.

"Take whatever you need," Voorhees said. "The motor pool is waiting for you. Don't forget you comm. We might need to communicate. Take how many men you need."

"I can do this myself," Moses said.

Voorhees leaned onto his desk. "You're damn good, Moses, but I don't have time for your cowboy shit."

"I don't need a team," Moses replied. "You need me to go down and assess the situation. I can do that better alone."

"Your team might become a strike force," Voorhees said.

"So, you're going to throw together a half-assed army of green fighters and conscript militia and march into a hornet's nest?"

"It's all we have," Voorhees admitted. "Besides, every person within the Perimeter pledged to defend this city. It's our hope and we're willing to die for it."

"You'll die alright," Moses replied. "And whoever is out there will get what they want, only easier. You have a city full of defenders, not gunmen."

"What do you suggest?"

"I know how these militias work," Moses said. "One person is driving the whole deal. About five others are waiting for their chance to take the reins. Take the leader out and the militia will disintegrate. That will give us more time."

"He's right," Uta added.

"So you're an assassin now?" Voorhees asked.

"I'm whatever it takes a gun to be," Moses said. "Give me a month. I'll find out who's behind all this and I'll take them out."

"We don't have a month."

Moses shrugged. "Then pay Uta to do his magic to slow them down"

"I couldn't do it any faster," Uta said. "I'd need time to gather ordinance. Besides, bombing isn't as accurate as Moses can be. He's your best bet."

"I'll get in, find out who runs the show then do the deed," Moses said.

"You make it sound so easy," Voorhees said.

"It's not, but you know I can do this. That's why you recruited me."

Voorhees stood and paced.

"This is Newlanta's future, Moses. Don't make me regret this."

"You won't," Moses said as he stood to leave. "Besides, if I screw it up neither of us will be around to be pissed about it."

Moses turned and strolled out of Voorhees's office before the commander could reply. He waited until he was outside before he grimaced. He knew all the Free Armies in South Georgia. He served with each one at some time in his life. There was only one that would be bold and ambitious enough to move on Newlanta, and he knew that squad best.

Zenobia's flat was empty when he arrived. He thought of packing his things then leaving a note, but he wanted to see her before he left. He didn't consider himself a sentimental person but he was fond of Zee. He sat, looking about the tiny room. They worked so hard for so little. At least it was honest work, with no killing or stealing. He changed his mind about waiting, searching the flat until he found a note pad and pencil.

"Next bath is on me," he wrote.

His next stop was the shop. The bay was filled as always, the mechanics focused on whatever equipment needed repair. Old Atlanta was once a major metropolis, a transportation hub that served the eastern region of the former USA. It teemed with wreckage, but only so much could be salvaged. Every piece of equipment has to be used, repaired and used again. A number of manufacturing plants existed outside the Perimeter but all were con-trolled by local militias or Free Armies too ignorant to revive them yet too strong to be forced out.

Moses went directly to Snake's office. The scruffy old man spat when he walked in.

"I don't know how in the hell you talked Voorhees into giving you a full kit," he said.

"His choice, not mine," Moses replied. "I just came for my dogs. Now shut up and give me the keys."

Snake reach over to the nearby wall and opened the key box. He snatched out the keys then threw them as hard as he could at Moses. Moses dodged them and they sailed through the shop and out the door. Moses grinned then flipped Snake a bird.

"I hope you die!" Snake shouted.

"I might just," Moses replied.

He knew better than to ask Snake where to find the truck. He'd find it in due time. For now, he wanted to claim his dogs. He picked up the keys then took a left through a pile of engine parts to Robotics. Esmerelda Rodrigues sat on a crate, peering through a magnifying glass as she soldered a circuit board. Her jet black hair was pulled up into a ponytail that teased her neck as she moved her head from side to side.

"Pritchard," she said without looking up.

"How do you do that?" he said.

"Do what?"

"Recognize me without seeing me."

"You have a distinct smell," she replied.

"Wow. That's cold."

Esmerelda placed down her soldering iron then removed her welding glasses to look at Moses. The glasses left an imprint between her light brown eyes and plump cheeks.

"You don't stink," she said. "I'm sensitive to pheromones."

"So, you're like a bloodhound."

Esmerelda frowned. "Fuck you."

"You wish."

They both laughed.

"Where are my dogs, Essie?"

"Call'em," she said.

"Frick! Frack!"

The dogs clattered from the storage area to Moses. They stopped a few feet away, scanning him before taking his side.

"Any upgrades?"

"I enhanced their targeting matrix and switched them to solar packs with increased capacity. They should run a good 72 hours before needing recharging."

Moses frowned. "That means longer down time."

"Where you been? In the Black?"

Esmerelda stood then waved for Moses to follow her. She led him to a pile of dingy components. Even in their worn state Moses was impressed. He kneeled before the stacks of salvaged parts, reaching for a battery. Esmerelda smacked his hand.

"No, sir. No touching the goodies."

"Where'd you get these?"

"Some hoarder passed through a few weeks ago," Esmerelda answered. "Voorhees tried to get him to stay but you know how they can be. He needed food and was willing to trade. He had no idea what he was carrying."

"So, my dogs can see better and run longer. What about weapon upgrades?"

Esmerelda strolled back to her work bench.

"You can't afford those. Besides, you're not authorized."

"Come on, Essie," he said. "We're friends."

"Not like that," she replied. "Now get out of my shop. I got work to do."

"Cool. I see how you are. No donuts for you."

Esmerelda laughed.

"Good hunting," she said. "Don't die."

Moses patted his leg and Frick and Frack followed him out the shop.

"I don't plan to, but you know what they say about plans."

Moses strolled to the lot, Frick and Frack trailing behind. He had no idea what vehicle he'd been assigned so he sought out the parking attendant, a young man with slick black hair and freckles.

"What am I driving?" he asked as he tossed the keys to the man. The man studied them then tossed them back.

"Green Dodge out back," he said. "Bike in the bed. And my name is Jaquan."

"Good to know," Moses said. As he was searching the lot a familiar voice interrupted him.

"So, you were going to leave without saying goodbye?"

Carmen, Zenobia's friend walked up to him, a smile on her face.

"Yep." He found the truck then opened the door to inspect the cabin. It was dingy and beat up.

"Zenobia deserves better than you," Carmen said.

Moses started the truck, inspecting the gauges. The speedometer was shot but at least the light switch worked.

"She does. You should tell her. She won't listen to me."

Carmen leaned into the cabin, grabbing his thigh. "Take me with you. I'm tired of Newlanta. I

used to be a Neutralizer so I can handle myself. And
we can amuse ourselves when things get slow."

Moses took Carmen's hand off his thigh, his
eyes narrow as he glared at Zenobia's so-called
friend.

"This is how you look out for your girl?"

Carmen grinned. "Zee's a grown ass woman.
She'll be alright. Besides, why do you care?"

Moses pushed Carmen away as he walked to
the rear of the truck.

"Frick! Frack!"

The dogs run up to him then jumped into the
truck bed, settling in beside the bike. Zeke walked
back to the truck cabin, climbed inside and
slammed the door. He glared at Carmen.

"I care."

Carmen stuck her head through the window.

"Do you love her? Because she loves you. All
she does is talk about you while you're gone. Then
you roll in, hit it, then leave."

"I don't love anyone...anymore," Moses replied.

Moses started the truck. The engine cranked
immediately, its mild chugging vibrating the worn
leather seats.

"Take me with you," Carmen shouted over
the engine noise.

"No." Moses shifted the truck into reverse.
"Too much trouble. Where I'm going is trouble
enough."

"I'll take that chance," Carmen replied.

Moses pressed the accelerator and the truck
rolled backwards.

"Bye Carmen. Tell your 'friend' Zenobia I
said goodbye."

"Fuck you!" Carmen shouted.

Moses laughed. "Second offer I've had today."

He pulled out of the parking shed and drove to the checkpoint. He handed his papers to Gilly, a pale man with an unruly head of red hair and squinty eyes.

"You're all set, killer," Gilly said. "Don't miss."

"I never do," Moses said.

He weaved the truck through the congested streets to the city's southside gates. The guards waved him through without checking his papers; few people were eager to leave Newlanta once they were granted entrance. It was those trying to enter that needed screening. He savored the good pavement near the city, knowing it was a luxury he'd lose very soon. Newlanta couldn't repair what it couldn't protect. The city controlled the land roughly twenty miles beyond the Perimeter Wall; more in the south and east, less in the north and west. The Appalachian mountain clans were too powerful and the much of the Westlands still burned. He'd have good road down to Stockbridge; beyond that the conditions depended on the strength and resources of whatever Free Army controlled the stretch he traveled. The truck would get him as far south as Macon; once there he's either sell it, trade it for ammo, or both. No good roads existed beyond Macon. Below the Sand Hills, known to the locals as 'The Gnat Line,' was chaos. It was the bloody crucible that made him who he was, the cauldron where he earned his reputation. He killed his first man at eight; by the time he reached puberty he was a skilled killer. At twenty he was being recruited or condemned by every Free Squad in old Georgia. He could name his price, but he learned none of them could give him what he wanted; peace.

He came close twice. One was when he fought with the Raptors; the second was Newlanta. The Raptors were a false hope, but Newlanta had the chance to be real. That's why he was driving south on I-75/85. To bring peace he had to handle the chaos of his past. He had to rejoin the Raptors, or at least that was the plan. He didn't know for sure, but he'd bet credits that they were the culprits behind the buildup. The problem was they might try to kill him as soon as they saw him. He didn't leave on good terms. But if they didn't, he'd have a chance to do what needed to be done.

Macon was an hour and half drive from Newlanta barring any interruption. There were always interruptions; feral cattle herds, beggars, ambushes; always something. So when he saw smoke rising about a mile ahead near the old Highway 16 exit, he wasn't surprised. Moses pulled off the highway, driving the truck into a stand of pines. He grabbed his sniper rifle, slung it across his back then stepped out the truck. Frick and Frack stirred.

"Stay," he said. The dogs settled down.

Moses entered the woods, working his way up a nearby hill for a better look. He took out his binoculars, focusing on the base of the smoke. What he saw caused his throat to tighten. He never got used to it, no matter how many times he saw it. Six bodies sprawled near a burning van, a family most likely. They were still fully clothed, which meant the ambush was recent. Whoever did it was probably lurking nearby, making sure they'd hit everyone. Moses placed his binoculars on the ground then brought his rifle to position. He loaded four rounds into the magazine then one in the chamber. He took a kneeling position, gripping the front of the rifle with his left hand and supporting it on his knee. He brought the scope to his eye, looking at the scene with the crosshairs. He held his breath and waited.

They came out of hiding minutes later, three men and one woman dressed in green jumpsuits and saucer-like helmets.

Doughboys, Moses thought. Real badasses.

Moses tracked them as they crept into the open. He waited for the sweetness, for that moment when they all paused. When it came, he squeezed off the rounds in quick succession, working the bolt action with flawless efficiency. Ten bodies lay in the road, four with one 30.06 round in their skulls. Moses waited until dusk before returning to the truck and continuing down the highway. He maneuvered around the wreckage and the bodies, sparing a glance at the hapless family. They were probably trying to reach Newlanta, hoping for safety and stability behind its formidable walls. How many others had died like them? He would tell Voorhees they needed to expand their sweeps. They would be invading warlord territory, but it was worth it if fewer innocent families were lost.

The Doughboys worried him. They were out of their range, much further north than he remembered. Shifting territory meant war, which meant he would have to be much more careful, if that was possible. He exited at Forsyth, or what used to be the small city. He pulled up behind the remains of a large department store, one he'd used long ago as a crash pad. If he was lucky it was still abandoned; if not, he would move on. He'd done enough killing for the day. Moses didn't bother unloading the truck except for the dogs.

"Security," he said.

While Frick and Frack trotted off Moses settled in. There would be no fire or any heat source this night just in case the Doughboys looking for their missing cohorts has sophisticated search tools. He wolfed down two cans of rations then unpacked his sleeping bag. As a precaution he draped the bag with a cold blanket to reduce his heat signal. Frick and Frack would alert him to any interlopers, so he settled in for a good sleep after a hard drive.

When he slept, he dreamed of the dead family. He saw them clearly, their fresh blood oozing into the asphalt. They sat up to look at him, their eyes brimming with tears. They touched their wounds, a look of confusion on their faces. Then they looked at him. Their mouths opened as they utter the same word.

"WHY?"

Moses sat up, tears in his eyes.

"I don't know," he whispered. "I don't know."

His link chip chirped, interrupting his grim thoughts. He found his eye piece and put it on. It took a minute for it to link with the dogs, another few seconds to display a visual. He counted six intruders. Four searched the warehouse while two rummaged his truck. The images weren't distinct, but Moses assumed they were more Doughboys. They probably found their buddies then began sniffing around. As much as he didn't want to, this would be wet work. They were too close for gunfire and he didn't want to attract any additional attention. He strapped on his knives then screwed suppressors on his handguns just in case.

Whoever they were, they were well trained. They worked the store in pairs, one point man, one back up. Moses knelt as he watched them, the cold blanket thrown over his shoulders.

"Eeny, meeny, miny, moe," he whispered. 'Mo' was the team approaching from his left.

Moses crept toward them. He found a metal bar as he worked his way toward the pair, stopping when he reached the interception point. He shifted his knife into his left hand and the bar into his right. Moses tossed the bar toward the team coming from his right. The quiet shattered as the bar crashed into a metal shelf then clattered to the floor. The right team halted and Moses grinned. They were very well trained; lesser soldiers would have sprayed the building with gunfire. The left team moved in, running toward the sound. Moses let the first man pass; he jumped up and grabbed the second man, his hand covering the man's mouth as he slit his throat. The first man spun about just in time to meet Moses face to face before Moses stabbed him in the throat as he took him down. Moses crouched by the dying men.

"We just want what's ours," a voice called out.

Moses didn't reply. They knew he knew their location; they were trying to find him. He checked his scanner; the men near the building entrance were probably listening for him as well. As much as he hated to do it, he armed the dogs.

"Your life for our loot," the voice continued. "It's a fair trade. That road kill was ours."

The words road kill made his hand shake with anger. It was a good thing Frick was in position; he activated and fired the homing rockets instinctively. The outside explosion was the perfect diversion. Moses was up and running toward his hunters before the shock subsided, a knife in each hand. This didn't have to be wet work; he wanted it to be.

He barrel rolled into both men, taking them down. He came up slashing and stabbing. The man closest to him died a bloody mess, the second man managed to fire a shot before Moses fell on him. His shot furrowed Moses's left thigh; he ignored the pain as he sliced and stabbed the man until he lay still. Moses limped toward the building entrance to see what was left of Frick and his truck.

His leg was throbbing by the time he reached the wreckage. Frick watched over the flaming vehicle, its rocket port still smoking. The other Doughboys sprawled nearby. Moses shook his head; two months rations up in smoke. There was nothing he could do about it except bandage his wound and move as soon as possible. The explosion and night fire would draw scavengers like flies to shit.

Moses opened Frick's first aid kit then treated his wound. He numbed the gash then set the dog on point for his next destination. It trotted into the night woods; Moses waited for ten minutes before following. His departure wasn't a moment too soon; as he entered the woods, he saw headlights approaching from the highway. Frack met him soon afterwards and together they followed Frick, the path meandering more than he remembered. A quick IR scan revealed why; Frick was avoiding scavengers converging on the explosion site from the east. Unless they were part of the same horde, there was bound to be a firefight.

Moses and Frick caught up with Frack at his backup hideaway, a dilapidated house hidden by kudzu, honeysuckle and blackberry vines. Years ago, he planted anti-personnel mines and heat sensors around it just in case he needed a place to hide and defend. He hoped they still worked. The dogs were programmed to walk through the death trap without triggering the ordinance. Moses trailed behind them until they reached the entrance to the kudzu covered shack. He pushed his way through the morass and was met by the pungent smell of decay.

"Great," he whispered. He turned on his torch, searching for the source of the smell. To his relief it was the carcass of either a coyote or a large dog. Moses settled into the opposite corner, curling against the damaged wooded wall as the dogs folded then shut down. In minutes he was deep into a dreamless sleep.

He awoke to the insistent vibration of his hip alarm. It was still dark, his chronometer displayed 5:00 a.m. Moses grabbed his HK MP5, slipping the clip under his body so not to make any noise. He lay still, listening for pursuers. The was no way they could sneak up on him; the vines, dead leaves and twigs revealed anything larger than a rabbit approaching. There was also no way out. He switched on his IR; there were fifteen heat signals moving his way. Moses crawled to Frick, opened its storage unit then took out the mine trigger.

Moses let them advance a few more seconds before pressing the manual detonation. The explosions deafened him as it jolted the shack. His ears were still ringing when the roof cracked and the sidewalls gave way. There was nothing he could do but curl up and pray the impact would not kill him. The support beam just missed his head, but the rear wall smashed his left foot. He choked back a scream as he struggled to load the clip into the HK.

"Fuck! It's a goddamn minefield!" someone said.

"Minefield hell," a woman answered. "Those charges were triggered."

"From where?"

The woman laughed. "There."

"If that bastard was inside that, his ass is dead. Whose still alive?"

"James, Diego you and me," the woman said.

"Shit! Let's get'em and get the fuck out of here. This shit is bound to draw flies."

Moses listened to the duo grunt as they lifted their wounded comrades then ran away. He waited until he was sure the interlopers were not turning back before testing his wound. He tried to sit then up but grimaced in pain. He waited until daylight had come and gone before dragging himself free of the wreckage and activating the dogs. Frack responded, debris sliding off its metal frame as it stood. Frick remained motionless. The dog had been damaged by the blasts. Moses didn't have the strength to dig the damaged dog free. He would have to leave it in hopes he could salvage it later.

Bodies surrounded the safe house, which wasn't good. Wolves, coyotes, panther cats and other scavengers would show up soon and none of them would have a problem putting down a meal that moved a little more than the carcasses they had come for. He tried to stand but as soon as he put weight on his injured foot he collapsed. There was no way he could enter a Free camp in his state; someone would try him for his gear as soon as he arrived. He'd have to find a place to heal. There was one option; easy to get in, hell to get out. He wouldn't play that card unless he absolutely had to.

He fashioned a brace for his foot then cut a sturdy branch from a nearby oak to use as a crutch. He packed on his gear then hobbled as far as he could from the destroyed cabin. He was a quarter of a mile away when he heard the howling, answered by the grating squeal of a panther cat. He picked up his pace the best he could. On a healthy foot he could cover seven to ten miles in a day; on his bad foot he barely made three. The last mile was torture. Moses realized he had no choice but to set up a permanent camp then let the healing nanos repair his foot. He found a steep hill that gave an unobstructed view of the surrounding area for at least 500 yards in every direction. An old observation hill most likely. The fact that it was unoccupied didn't say much, but Moses had no choice. If someone or something was going to come for him, he wasn't going to make it easy. He struggled up the hill for most of the day, Frack trailing behind. Once he reached the summit, he set up his lean-to. There would be no fire on this night as well; he'd have to make do once again with cold rations.

It took three days for his foot to heal, even with the nanos. He hated using them; they were Old tech and extremely rare. He doubted he would be able to replace them, but he had no choice. The mission had to proceed.

"You're getting old, boss man," he said as he tried his foot on the fourth day. There was slight pain but nothing he couldn't handle. Once he reached Macon he would rent a shell and rest a few more days. The warlord controlling the city did her best to be fair-minded, as least as fair as a warlord could be. He still had blood on his hands; maybe it had been forgotten over the years.

Three days into his journey his plans for Macon became a bust. Moses looked upon the city from an old billboard that occupied the crest of a steep hill. Doughboys patrolled the outskirts; columns of smoke swirled into the sky from various sections of the city. It was a full-scale raid. Moses lowered his binoculars then spit. He would have to find a way around. Cutting through would most likely mean running into raiders, and he wasn't healed enough for a firefight. He linked visuals to Frack then switched the robotic canine to stealth reconnaissance. It would drain Frack's batteries, but it was a necessary precaution. He set the range at five miles, which put Frack a half a day ahead of him. In the meantime, he would wait and heal. Frack set out at a trot; Moses set visuals on standby as he checked out his surroundings.

He found a dense stand of pines and oaks then set up camp. The nearby homes looked weathered yet inviting, but if he knew anything about the Doughboys it was that they were very thorough. He gazed through Frack's sensors at the damage being wrought, bracing himself for the worst. It was bad, but not as bad as he anticipated. They were taking captives, killing only those who resisted. Most interesting was they were taking special care not to harm anyone. That was way out of character for Doughboys. He didn't know them to be slavers; someone must be paying a good price for bodies and it seemed the Doughboys had adapted.

Moses wanted to help but it would be foolish for him to try. He had an assignment, and he was only one man. But sometimes, no matter how a person tries to avoid trouble, it finds its way to you.

The screams came from his left as he was packing the last of his gear. Moses loaded his HK and attached the suppressor as the voices grew louder. The family burst out into the open, running down the middle of the street with four Doughboys in pursuit. Moses watched the drama for a moment, struggling with himself on what to do. Shooting the Doughboys, suppressor or not, would reveal his position. Not shooting them would result in the family taken as slaves. If he was near Newlanta the decision would be easy. But out in the Wild, the situation was different.

"Fuck it," he said.

Moses gunned down the Doughboys. The fleeing family froze, looking at the dead men in terror. Moses emerged from his hiding place.

"Over here!" he shouted.

The family stared at him, then ran.

"Shit," he whispered.

He heard more voices. As he suspected more Doughboys were coming. If the family had heeded his call they would be safely hidden. But he couldn't blame them. With what they were going through he was just another threat. He strolled into the open, checking his weapons along the way. If he couldn't save them, the least he could do was be a serious distraction.

He did a quick search of the bodies and found three hand grenades. He took one of the Doughboy helmets, put it on his head then waited. Minutes later twelve Doughboys ran toward him.

"What's going on?" the lead man shouted. "How many?"

Moses answered by tossing the grenades.

"What the . . ."

Moses flattened as the charges exploded. Then he was up in the kneeling position, spraying the smoke with automatic fire. He waited for the air to clear before moving. He wanted to make sure if anyone was still alive, they would follow him. More footsteps and shouts came his way. He could say one thing; Doughboys weren't ones to run from a fight. After he was done with them they would wish they had.

Moses waited until he was sure the other Doughboys had seen him before he sprinted for the cover of a nearby neighborhood. The homes were barely livable, but these days they were better than most. He found a house that gave him a clear view of the road then took off his guns, loading each with a fresh clip. He was using a lot of ammo, but he'd make up for it later.

The Doughboys appeared moments later. The soldiers separated, some investigating and relieving their dead comrades of their gear, the others scanning the area for him. Moses waited until the Doughboys were packed in the road before opening fire. They scattered; some running in his direction. Others took cover and fired wildly; a few rounds bounced off the walls of his hideout. Once everyone had taken cover he worked away from where the family fled. Once he had the Doughboys's full attention he strapped on his guns then ran south, following the electronic trail Frack left for him. The Doughboys pursued him for five miles before giving up the chase. They were there for slaves; dead men don't get paid.

Moses kept up a brisk pace until he was a few miles south of Macon. He found another wooded spot near a slow-moving creek then sat to rest. He was tired and hungry. He decided he wanted fresh meat, so he took out his hand line, dug up a few worms from the nearby vegetation and fished. He caught a bass, two bream and a catfish, more than enough for a good meal. He cleaned the fish then started a small fire. He gathered lemongrass and blackberries then leaned on a pine tree for a tasty meal. As he settled in for a good sleep Frack returned. Moses put on his eyepiece then accessed the dog's recorder. He smiled at the images. What he and Uta suspected was true. His old friends were still in business. Moses continued to study the data and discovered another surprise.

"I'll be damned," he said. A smile came to his face as he continued to watch. He now knew his destination, but a detour was in order. Tomorrow the real fun would begin.

- 3 -

The scent of peaches drifted on the humid air, causing Moses mouth to water. He picked a few to add to his pouch then hurried back on the paved road leading to Fox Valley. It was early morning and he was thankful for the break from the heat. Frack paced nearby yet out of sight, using the woods and other vegetation for cover. He usually kept the dogs on a loose leash, taking advantage of the observation tech and keeping them away just in case things got tight. He missed Frick, but he didn't have time to repair the unit. He checked the homing signal; the dog was still in place, running on low power. Fortunately, no one had found the unit and stripped it of useful tech. Without his command box the dog would be useless to anyone except a skilled hack tech.

Someone had pacified the region. It was probably the same someone who now had the Doughboys on a leash. That could be a good or bad situation, depending on how the pacification occurred. Knowing the warlords, it was probably bad.

So far, he hadn't had to avoid any patrols or check-points, so the signs were encouraging despite what he witnessed in Macon. A thought came to him which made him laugh out loud. Was the peace his parents dreamed of on the horizon? His question was answered by a vehicle breaking the skyline before him. As it came closer Moses spotted the machine gun mounted on the hood. It was too late for him to seek cover; he dropped the peach then checked his weapons.

The vehicle was in range but didn't fire. Moses kept walking, glancing left to right for others. Frack was silent. The vehicle slowed to a stop and a dark brown woman jumped from the passenger side. She wore a uniform Moses didn't recognized, dark blue with a yellow collar, a blue cap with a wildcat symbol embraided in the center. She wore a Glock strapped to her waist and an AR-15 slung across her back. The woman stopped a few feet in front of him then took off her hat before speaking.

"Good morning," the woman said.

Moses nodded. "Good morning."

The woman extended her hand. Moses took it and they shook.

"I'm Officer Bleek," the woman said. "Welcome to the Fox Valley Protectorate."

"So that's what they're calling this now," Moses replied. "Moses Pritchard."

"You've been here before?" Bleek asked.

"Grew up here," Moses replied. "Back when it was a lot less organized."

"Things have changed," Officer Bleek said. The officer nodded at his rifle strapped across his chest then at the sidearms on his hips.

"That's a lot of guns."

"I'm a gunman," Moses said.

The officer's smile faded.

"We don't have a need for your kind in Fox Valley," she said.

Moses frowned. "Now that's not friendly."

"You're welcomed to visit, but you'll have to check those." Bleek nodded at his weapons.

"I got no problem with that. I'm anxious for a little Fox Valley hospitality and I need the rest."

The officer's smile returned. "In that case, hop in. We'll give you a ride. And you're going to have to pay for those peaches."

The jaunt to Fox Valley took twenty minutes. The good pavement gave out just before they reached the town, but the red clay road was smooth and well maintained. There was no wall protecting the city, just a double fence crowned with razor wire. It wouldn't last a minute in a heavy firefight, but most settlements outside of Newlanta wouldn't. Most people prepared and prayed, hoping such an attack would never come and if it did, they would have fair enough warning to flee and take their chances in the bush.

The vehicle pulled up to the gate and the guards waved them through. Both stared at Moses as they drove by and he smiled and waved back.

"So you're a smart ass, too," Bleek said.

"It's one of my endearing traits," Moses replied.

"I suggest you keep it in check when you meet the mayor."

"I'll do my best."

The paved road returned as they entered Fox Valley. The 19th century buildings had been repaired and now served as shops and homes for the inhabitants. Moses had to give it to the Elders; they knew how to build things that lasted. They sped through the town, slowing for railroad tracks that hadn't seen activity in centuries. The town center was a cluster of brick buildings surrounding a roundabout. A pedestal ringed by red azaleas occupied in the center. The statue that once stood on the pedestal was long gone, its only remnants a weathered pair of shoes. They veered left then followed the road to a white antebellum home with a gravel parking lot.

"Here we are," Bleek said. "Follow me."

Moses did as he was told as he surveyed the town. There wasn't much security, which meant the mayor was in good terms with the nearby warlords. He or she must be supplying something of mutual benefit for them all. Moses thought about the Macon raid, the well-groomed peach fields and put two and two together. As he entered the building his mood had become grim.

A large man with a bald head stuffed in a Fox Valley officer uniform stood behind his desk as they entered.

"Koots," Bleek said. "The man here needs to check his guns."

The man gave Moses a hard stare. Moses smirked as he began taking off his guns and placing them on the desktop. Koots tagged each of the weapons then placed them in a nearby gun cabinet.

"I won't be here long," Moses said. "When I leave, I want every last one of my guns. If one's missing, you and I will have words."

The man was about to laugh when Moses shot across the gap between them then locked the man in a chokehold. Koots clawed at his forearms, gasping from breath. Bleek and the other officer were about to draw their weapons, but Moses let

Koots go, shoving his head into the desk. The man fell unconscious to the floor.

"What's going on out here!"

The door behind the man opened and a tall woman with dark brown skin and a short afro entered the room with a stern look on her face. Moses recognized her immediately.

"Shakira Mfumu?"

Shakira glared at Moses for a moment then smiled.

"Well I'll be damned! Moses Pritchard is still alive!"

"At least for now," Moses replied.

They hugged, Shakira pounding his back with her fists before letting him go.

"I got this, Bleek," she said. "Take Koots to the infirmary."

Bleek and the other officer struggled to get Koots off the floor then dragged him out of the office.

"Come on in, Killer."

Moses followed Shakira into the office. Unlike Voorhees, her office was well appointed. She sat behind a large mahogany desk in a refurbished high back leather chair. She offered Moses a seat.

"So where the hell you been?" Shakira asked.

"Newlanta."

Shakira clapped her hand.

"I knew it! I remember the last conversation we had. You sounded like you were done with this shit."

"I thought I was," Moses lied. "But I got bored. So here I am."

"Once a killer, always a killer," Shakira said.

"What about you?" Moses asked. "Mayor of Fox Valley?"

"You weren't the only one fed up," Shakira said. "As a matter of fact, it was you leaving that gave me the idea."

"But slaving?" Moses said. "Really, Shakira?"

Shakira's jovial mood vanished.

"You know the drill, killer. If you're not useful you're dead. I know you haven't been behind those walls jacking off."

"I've had to use my skills from time to time."

"Exactly!" Shakira stood and began to pace.

"Jamal looked high and low for you," she said. "If he had found you he would have killed you."

"Tried to kill me," Moses corrected her.

"Still an arrogant asshole," Shakira said. "I took off a few months later. Couldn't head north to Newlanta; you left a trail and Jamal was watching so I went west. Found these folks in Fox Valley trying to make a go of it on their own and volunteered to protect them. While I was here I got some ideas on how they could improve their lot and buy a little safety as well."

"By slaving?"

"It ain't that simple," Shakira said. "We don't hunt slaves, we buy'em. Well, we barter for them. The warlords give us the labor and in exchange we give them food from our farms. We're kind of a neutral zone. Nobody messes with us because they need to eat."

Moses looked and Shakira, disapproval on his face.

"Don't look at me like that," she said. "We do what we got to do."

Moses couldn't go to war with Fox Valley. He had other things to do but he made a note to pay his friend Shakira a visit later.

"So, can I stay the night?"

Shakira grinned. "Of course. I have a bunk in my office."

"Can I have my guns back?"

"Nope," Shakira said. "Rules are rules."

"You made the rules. You can break them."

"I can, but I won't. I know you, remember?"

Shakira stood then walked to the door.

"Come on. Let's get you something to eat then get you settled in. You can stay as long as you like."

"One night will do," Moses said.

"Why you in such a hurry? You got somewhere to be?"

Moses didn't answer.

"Oh, you're shy now," Shakira joked.

"The less you know, the better off you are," Moses said.

They left the office. A new officer sat at the desk, watching Moses warily as he sauntered by.

"We'll walk," Shakira said. "Deedee's is not that far."

"Deedee's?"

It's a restaurant. Good home cooked food."

Fox Valley must be prospering if a person could afford to open a business. There were very few in Newlanta.

They strolled through the roundabout then two buildings down to Deedee's. The aroma hit Moses and he was suddenly famished. They entered the restaurant, a bell ringing as the door swung wide. Four tables with a pair of chairs sat near the front door. The restaurant was empty. Shakira took a seat and Moses followed.

"Hey Deedee!" she shouted. "You got customers!"

"I'm coming, I'm coming!" a high-pitched voice shouted back.

Deedee entered the restaurant from the back like a sunrise on a perfect day. Moses couldn't remember seeing a person so vibrant in his thirty-two years. The tall, light brown skinned woman wore an apron covering her slim body from neck to knees, wiping her hands with a towel as she walked to their table.

"My first customers of the day!" she said.

"Happy as always," Shakira replied.

"I'm happy because you brought a stranger," Deedee replied. "A paying stranger, I hope."

Shakira shared a mock frown.

"So I'm invisible?"

"You don't pay," Deedee replied.

"Pleased to meet you, Miss Deedee," Moses said.

"And he's polite too!" Deedee said.

"What passes for money around here?" Moses asked.

"I could use some shotgun shells," Deedee said.

"You got the right person," Shakira replied. "Moses here is a gunman."

"That doesn't mean I have shotgun shells."

Shakira gave him the side-eye. "Do you?"

Moses laughed. "Yep."

Deedee reached behind her head to tighten her head scarf.

"Four shells will get you both a good meal. I got grits, bacon, eggs and biscuits out back."

"No rations?" Moses joked.

"Get out of my restaurant!" Deedee said.

They both laughed while Shakira glanced between them.

"I sure would like to eat before you two get to the serious flirting," Shakira said.

"I'll be back with your plates," Deedee said.

Moses leaned his chair back, balancing it on the back legs.

"So what's your status?"

"We got about five hundred people counting the slaves . . . I mean laborers. Cesspools and out-houses mainly, but we're working on plumbing. If we could find a decent engineer, we could build a hydro plant on the Flint River and start generating some electricity."

"What about protection?"

"Ten officers."

Moses sucked his teeth. "That ain't shit."

"Who you telling?" Shakira replied. "Hard to find folks willing to do what we do, even if they're vulnerable. And the ones that volunteer are usually crazy."

Deedee returned with their plates. Moses couldn't remember ever seeing a plate of food more inviting. He tasted everything and closed his eyes in pleasure.

"I didn't know food could taste this good," he said.

"Fresh off the farm," Deedee said. "You should come back for supper."

"I most definitely will." He looked at Shakira. "You hiring?"

Shakira laughed as she crumbled her bacon into her grits.

"You'll work for food?" she said.

"Yes ma'am!"

Moses and Shakira finished their meals then Moses gave Miss Deedee five shells instead of four, which she gladly accepted.

Shakira and Moses took a stroll through Fox Valley. Technically the town was far behind New-lanta, but the growing metropolis could use the Valley's food source. And then there was the slave issue. Voorhees would be totally against it, but Moses felt Shakira could be persuaded to give it up as long as she was protected from the local warlords.

He was getting distracted again. He needed to focus on the business at hand.

"I could really use that bed you promised."

Shakira winked. "No problem."

Shakira took him back to her office. She opened the door behind her desk. There was a bed, a small dresser and a sink inside.

"Long days?" Moses asked.

Shakira shrugged. "Sometimes."

Moses sat on the edge of the bed and pulled off his boots.

"I'll be back around evening," Shakira said. "We'll hit Deedee's for supper."

"Sounds like a plan."

Moses laid back on the bed as Shakira closed the door.

"See you in a few."

It seemed as if he'd barely closed his eyes before the door opened.

"Moses."

Moses sat up, rubbing his eyes. Shakira stood in the doorway.

"Get up. We got trouble."

Moses's eyes cleared to Shakira's worried expression.

"Who?"

"Doughboys."

Moses put on his boots.

"My guns?"

"You got'em. I got a feeling this has something to do with you."

Moses didn't answer.

"Shit, killer!" Shakira said. "What the hell did you do? The Doughboys's ain't never come here strapped."

"A few of them got in my way on the way down," Moses said, his voice calm.

"You're in some real shit then," Shakira said. "If you got beef with the Doughboys, you got beef with Jamal."

So now he knew who they were working for.

"They're fishing," Moses said. "They never saw me."

"You should probably stay here just in case, but I need you because things might get ugly."

"You got it," Moses said.

Moses followed Shakira to the gun cabinet. She opened the metal cabinet, took out her AR-15 then stepped aside. Moses gathered his guns then strapped them on. They slapped each other's shoulders.

"We got this," Shakira said.

"Every day," Moses replied.

Shakira and Moses walked out of the office together. Shakira touched her communicator on her ear.

"Where are the Doughboys, Bleek?"

"At the roundabout."

"What?!? Who let them in?"

"Who was going to stop them? They brought armor."

Shakira cut her eyes at Moses. Moses shrugged.

"Looks like you better contact Jamal."

Shakira tapped her communicator twice.

"Yes . . . Jamal please . . . Hi Jamal, it's Shakira Everett from Fox Valley. Why the fuck are the Doughboys in my city with armor? Is there something you need to tell me, because I can stop this shipment of beef to Robbins right now . . . You'll take care of it? When . . . That's not soon enough . . . We'll be waiting. Out."

"So what's up?" Moses asked.

"He said he'll handle it."

"How long is that going to take?"

"I don't know."

Moses replaced the AR-15 clip with a different clip from his pack.

"What's in that?" Shakira asked.

"Armor piercing rounds," Moses said. "Made them myself."

Shakira rolled her eyes. "Don't tell my you're about to have a shootout with a tank?"

Moses grinned. "You know me. I'm always prepared."

"Yeah, but the rest of us aren't. Give me ten to get behind a building before you start blasting."

"This is your show," Moses said. "I'm following your lead. Just wanted to let you know I got you."

"Shit. I'm stuck between you and the Doughboys."

As they approached the roundabout Moses felt better. What the guards had described as armor was a plated Hummer with a 20mm cannon mounted on the roof. It was formidable, but he could handle it. Twenty Doughboys milled around the vehicle, paying close attention to the surrounding buildings. They focused on Moses and Shakira as they neared the roundabout, pulling their weapons closer. One of Doughboys, a wide man wearing a dingy white shirt and fatigue pants with suspenders came to them with a predatory smile on his face. He extended his hand. Shakira didn't take it.

"Commander Alexi Romano," the man said.

Shakira looked the man up and down.

"Shakira. What the fuck are you doing here, Romano?"

"We're looking for a rogue gunman," Romano answered. "Ambushed a team in Forsyth then interrupted a collection in Macon."

"And why would you think he would come here?" Shakira asked.

"Why not?" Romano replied. "Whoever it is might need to eat, and you got plenty of food. Besides, we're looking out for you. It's not like you're strapped."

Shakira nodded at Moses. "We're fine. We don't need you babysitting us. Now go."

"We'd like to look around," Romano said.

"No," Shakira replied.

Romano folded his arms. "Sounds like you have something, or someone, to hide."

"How the hell did you get to be a commander? Why in the broken world would we want to harass Doughboys?"

"Maybe this rogue is someone you know." Romano's eyes lingered on Moses.

Shakira sighed. "Just so you know, I contacted Jamal. If his next commissary shipment is 'delayed,' he'll know why."

Moses could see where this was going. Alexi was using his interference as an excuse to make a play for Fox Valley. When it came down to it, Jamal probably didn't care who controlled the farmlands as long as the supplies kept flowing. Neither did the other warlords. In addition, he controlled Romano.

Shakira was a deserter, just like him. He glanced toward Shakira; the look in her eyes told him she'd just come to the same conclusion.

"Fuck it," Shakira said.

She blasted Romano in his chest with her automatic then turned her weapon on the other Doughboys. As they ducked for cover Moses unloaded his gun on the Humvee, riddling the vehicle with holes. One of the Doughboys tried to man the 20mm but Moses sprayed him before he could load. Moses and Shakira fell quickly into retreat and cover mode, as they fled for the cover of the nearby buildings.

"No dammit, don't come in!" he heard Shakira shout into her communicator. "Get your asses to the gate and make sure no more of these motherfuckers get through. We got this."

"*We do?*" Moses thought.

He took a quick peek. The Doughboys were holding position, probably waiting for someone among them to assume command since Romano laid sprawled in the street bleeding out. Two Doughboys sprinted toward them but Moses sent them running back for cover with two short bursts from his HK.

"You should have killed them!" Shakira shouted.

"No need to," Moses shouted back. "I think you killed their inspiration."

Moses sprinted to Shakira then reloaded. He was about to speak when Beek's voice blared from Shakira's mike.

"Boss! We got a chopper coming in low and hot."

"Take it down!" Shakira shouted.

"Too late," Bleek replied. "It was over and past us before we could aim. It's on you."

Shakira punched the wall; Moses took the clip out of his rifle then reloaded with another from his pack. He looked at Shakira and winked.

"Anti-aircraft rounds. We're good," he said.

"Is there anything you're not prepared for?" she asked.

"It better not be," he replied.

The shooting subsided as the sound of the chopper increased. Moses peeked over the wall to see the two-person craft hover for a moment over the roundabout then land. The rotors slowed then stopped as the doors swung open. The pilot stepped out first, a 9mm in her hand, a cap pulled low over her head, her dreads brushing the shoulders of her black flight jumpsuit. The passenger stepped out moments later, a tall heavy-set man in green fatigues wearing a cap and mirror shades. Moses looked at the hulking figure and grinned.

"Jamal Watkins," he said.

"This just keeps getting better and better," Shakira replied.

If Jamal was in the middle of Fox Valley it meant that a heavy force was not far away. Everyone in the city knew better than to continue shooting. The warlord took off his shades revealing his hazel eyes then scanned the area as if he was sizing up property for a new home. He removed his cap then ran his hand over his bald head, the light brown skin of his head slightly lighter than the rest of his body. Standing next to the much shorter chopper pilot made him seem taller.

"Well this is a mess," Jamal said with a deep, resonant voice that carried throughout the roundabout. "I'm going to need everyone to come out so we can figure out what the hell is going on."

The Doughboys emerged from hiding immediately, gathering around their commander. Shakira and Moses locked eyes.

"You ready for this?" Moses asked.

"Me? I'm good. I'm not the one he was trying to kill. You know you could make a run for it."

Moses shook his head. "No. This is what I wanted, just a little sooner than I planned."

"You must have a death wish," Shakira said.

Moses grinned. Something like that."

"It's your funeral," Shakira replied.

They stepped from behind the wall together, guns raised. Jamal tucked his shades into his shirt pocket then smiled.

"Shakira. Is this the way to greet a friend?"

"No," Shakira replied. "But I'm not your friend."

Jamal covered his heart with both hands. "That hurt, Shakira. I always considered you . . ."

Jamal's fake smile faded as his eyes focused on Moses.

"I'll be damned. Moses Pritchard."

Moses nodded. "Jamal. How you been?"

Jamal folded his arms across his chest. Shakira and Moses stopped a few feet away from the chopper.

"Never thought I'd see you again," Jamal said.

"Same here. We didn't end on the best of terms."

"That's an understatement."

Jamal glared at Shakira. She shrugged.

"I was just as surprised as you are," she said.

Jamal forced a smile. "So what dragged you out of Newlanta?"

Moses couldn't hide his surprise.

"Yeah, I knew where you were," Jamal continued. "Voorhees is not the only one who has eyes."

So Voorhees was right. Jamal had his sights on Newlanta. He also had contacts in Newlanta. For what, he wasn't sure. His relationship with Fox Valley seemed to be friendly, at least for the moment. Maybe he was looking for some kind of alliance. That was doubtful but still a possibility.

"I got bored," Moses replied.

"I could see that," Jamal said. "Rescuing tree trash could get a little tiring. Although I'll have to admit I'm impressed by Voorhees's little experiment."

"I hate to interrupt, but let's talk about the Doughboys," Shakira said. "Did you have anything to do with this shit?"

"Of course not," Jamal replied. "We have an agreement, but they're not completely under my control. You know how that goes, don't you Moses?"

"She's not talking about me," Moses replied.

Jamal sucked his teeth. He walked over to Romano's body then squatted beside it.

"Romano. I should have known. He's been bucking for bigger things for a minute now. Asked for the Macon assignment. I guess he decided to grab for a bigger piece of the pie."

Jamal stood.

"You actually did me a favor on this one," he continued. "This won't happen again. What you do here is valuable to me and everyone else in the region. The time is coming when the fighting will end and we can finally focus on rebuilding this state.

Maybe even the country. Your work here will be a pillar of the coming prosperity."

"I'll believe that when I see it," Shakira replied. "In the meantime, keep your boots off my property."

Jamal nodded. "I'll do my best." He shifted his eyes from Shakira to Moses.

"Moses, I'll be seeing you soon?"

"You might," Moses replied.

"I hope so. I can always use a good gunman, and you're still the best. At least that's what I hear."

"What happened to all that talk about the fighting ending?" Moses said.

Jamal smiled. "It hasn't ended yet. Until then it's a gunman's peace. See you soon."

Jamal approached one of the Doughboys. The woman saluted him then turn to the others.

"Let's go!" she shouted.

The Doughboys gathered their dead and wounded, loaded them into their remaining vehicles then drove away. Jamal and the pilot climbed into the chopper then lifted off, Shakira and Moses covering their faces from the swirling debris. They watched as the chopper faded into the distance.

Shakira touched her communicator.

"Bleek!"

"Ma'am?"

"Track the Doughboys and make sure they don't double back."

"Yes ma'am."

She took a few minutes to take a head count. She didn't lose anyone, which was damn lucky. Moses observed her with a smile on his face. His friend had become a decent administrator since he last saw her. It seemed everyone wanted the world to change.

"Everybody go home," she said. "You deserve the rest. Fox Valley can stand a few hours without us. Report back to duty in the morning."

The officers let out a weak cheer then headed in different directions. Shakira watched them for a minute before turning to Moses.

"You know that wasn't an invitation," she said as she walked up to him. "It was an order."

Moses checked his guns.

"I know," he replied.

"You going?"

"Yep."

"You're walking into the lion's den."

"Seems so."

Shakira gripped his shoulder, massaging them.

"I could use a few shots. How about you?"

"Definitely," Moses answered. "What you got in this town?"

"Come on. I'll take you to The Still."

They sauntered from the roundabout as the citizens emerged from hiding. Shakira waved off the curious; Moses smiled and nodded. They were crossing the street to the shops when Frack trotted up the middle of the thoroughfare. Shakira raised her automatic but Moses grabbed the barrel and pulled it down.

"It's mine," he said.

Shakira looked at him then rolled her eyes.

"Just couldn't get a normal dog, could you?"

"Normal dogs don't come with solar charge panels, laser sights and rockets," Moses answered.

Frack fell into step with them as Moses downloaded its info.

"Newlanta is pretty advance if they're sending you into the field with this kind of equipment," Shakira commented.

"It is," Moses said. "Which is why you should contact Voorhees. You're a valuable asset, and they have tech that could help you upgrade this hick town."

Shakira shoved him. "It's my hick town. You recruiting?"

Moses grinned. "Sort of."

"I like being neutral," Shakira replied. "It's good not to be on anybody's side."

"I have a feeling the time of being neutral is coming to an end," Moses said.

She stopped before a storefront with no sign. "Here we are!"

The Still's interior didn't vary much from Deedee's; well-worn tables with wooden chairs scattered about, a bar with a dingy mirror hanging on the wall behind it. A scruffy brown man wearing a white shirt and jeans emerged from the back as they entered.

"Hey, Shakira. I figured you'd be along when I heard all the shooting," the man said.

"Hey Tito," Shakira replied. "Either that or you'd have a new mayor."

"I'm glad they missed." Tito nodded at Moses. "Who's your friend?"

Moses walked up to Tito then shook his hand.

"Moses Pritchard."

"Tito Puentes."

"He's from Newlanta," Shakira said.

Tito folded his arms as he sized up Moses. "You come to lead us to the promised land?"

69

Moses laughed. "I'm just here for the food and liquor."

Tito smiled. "Then you came to the right place."

Moses noticed Shakira's hands shaking as he sat down. She looked up at him and grinned.

"Yeah, ain't that a bitch," she said.

"You should have said something," Moses replied.

"And punk out in front of my favorite killer? Nah. Gave me a chance to feel brave again."

"That wasn't brave," Moses said. "That was stupid. You could have gotten us both killed."

"Couldn't miss at that range," Shakira said.

Moses's anger subsided. He placed his hand on Shakira's.

"I'm sorry. Is this why you left Jamal?"

"Yeah. And it's the reason why he didn't bother dragging me back. I'm a better farmer than a killer now. Still, I shoot better than most."

Tito came to the table with popcorn, a bottle of moonshine and two shot glasses.

"It's on the house," he said.

"Good man!" Shakira replied.

Moses filled the glasses and they drank shots until they were drunk. They left The Still then staggered to Deedee's, who held the door open as they entered.

"We're hungry!" Moses shouted.

"I'll fix y'all a plate to go," Deedee said.

"We want to eat here," Shakira replied.

"No hell you won't," Deedee replied. "Y'all are coming from The Still. I'm not gonna have you throwing up in my restaurant."

They sat at an empty table, the other patrons smiling and raising their glasses to them. It felt good to protect people, to make sure they were safe. Moses reflected on his past, on the times when he lived in the Wild with his family. It was just the three of them, doing the best they could against the Dark, which is what mama called it. Despite the chance they were being deceived his parents never hesitated to help anyone they came across, sharing food, ammo, medicine, whatever they could spare. He asked his mama one day why they did that.

"We ain't never gonna see these folks again mama," he said. "Why we helping them?"

"We're planting seeds," mama said. "You're right. We probably won't see them again. But maybe the kindness we showed them they'll show to someone else. And maybe one day we all will be helping each other and all this fighting will end."

Mama's memory sobered him. By the time Deedee arrived with the food he was solemn.

"You alright?" she asked.

"I'm fine," Moses replied. "How much?"

Deedee waved. "On the house. Y'all chased the bad guys away again. That's payment enough."

Moses and Shakira took their meals outside and ate in silence sitting on the sidewalk, each dealing with their own thoughts.

"You can bunk in my office," Shakira said.

"Thanks," Moses replied.

"You crashing?" Shakira asked.

Moses grinned. "Yeah."

"You never get used to it, do you?"

"Nope."

"Helps when you have somebody."

"For some," Moses said.

"You know, Deedee seems to like you."

Moses shook his head. "I'm okay. Besides, I just met the woman, and she just met me."

Shakira laughed. "That's the Moses I know. Damn prude. You better get it while it wants to be got."

"You live your life, I'll live mine," Moses said.

They finished their meals then strolled to Shakira's office. Shakira unlocked the office then stepped aside.

"You know where it is," she said. "I'll see you in the morning."

"Thanks. I'm going to need a ride. Can you spare one?"

"Why don't you ride that robot dog?"

Moses chuckled. "That's not what it's for. Do you have something?"

"I'll see what I can do. G'night, killer."

"Night."

Moses took off his gear, washed up then sat on the edge of the bed. Shakira was right; you never get used to it. The drinking and sexing took the edge off, but it was always there. According to papa that was a good sign. It meant you were still human. He said the day you stopped feeling was the day you became a monster. The world didn't need any more monsters.

Moses lay back on the hard mattress, fighting his demons until fatigue won out and he fell asleep.

- 4 -

Morning came too soon as it always did. Moses opened his eyes to muted sunlight stealing through the thin window curtains. He eased out of bed, his old injuries giving him more aches than normal. He wasn't old, but he'd been through more than most and his body reminded him every morning, especially in the winter. Good thing it was late summer, otherwise he'd be semi-paralyzed. He reached for his pack then took out his pill case. He frowned when he looked inside. He had three painkillers remaining and couldn't get any more until he returned to Newlanta.

"Shit," he said. He closed the case and shoved it back in his pack.

He washed up. By the time he finished he heard the office door open.

"Morning, Moses!" Shakira shouted.

Moses sauntered into the office.

"Hey!" he said.

They hugged, patting each other on the pack.

"You sleep good?" Shakira asked.

"Good enough," Moses replied. "You got that ride for me?"

"Still working on it. Come on, let's get some breakfast."

Deedee greeted them with a smile and pancakes. Moses poured the sorghum syrup over his while shaking his head.

"I must be a fool for leaving," he said.

"You are," Shakira replied. "Last chance, killer. Take the ride I'm giving you and head the other way."

"Can't do that," Moses said with a mouth full of pancakes. "The man asked for me to come see him, so I'm going."

Shakira cut her pancakes into small cubes before smothering them with syrup.

"You're walking into a trap."

"I know," Moses said.

"He's going to kill you."

"I don't think so," Moses replied. "If I know one thing about Jamal, it's that everything has a price. He's not angry with me because I left; he's angry with me because he felt he didn't get his money's worth. I'll cut him a deal, maybe work for him a few months for just room and board and he'll be okay."

"Oh, you think so?"

Moses took a big swig of water. "I know so. Why do you think Fox Valley is still here?"

Shakira nodded. "I see your point. But I'm a washed-up killer with a town full of food."

"I appreciate your concern," Moses said. "But I'll be okay. Besides, I need to get inside."

"Don't tell me," Shakira said. "I don't want to know."

"Then stop worrying about me and eat your breakfast."

They finished their meals then Shakira took Moses to the mechanics shed. The large barn was surrounded by rusted vehicles of all kinds and a few that were in not-so-bad condition.

"Lee!" Shakira shouted.

A young woman stood up, her head just clearing one of the car carcasses. Grease stained her brown dimpled cheeks, a dingy baseball cape covering most of her braids. She waved, a wrench in her hand.

"Hey, Shakira!"

"Hey, Monica. Where's Lee?"

"She's in the barn getting the bike ready."

Moses frowned. "Bike? You're giving me a damn bike?"

"Calm down," Shakira replied. "You'll be happy. Trust me."

They walked by Monica, the woman looking at Shakira with a dreamy look on his face.

"Looks like somebody has a crush on you," Moses said.

"It's way beyond that," Shakira said. "That was my last night. The woman's got talent."

The woman Moses assumed was Lee squatted beside a dirt bike. She stood, facing them in dingy coveralls, a worn baseball cap on her head. She wiped her hands before shaking Shakira's hand.

"Thank you for making my best worker late," she said to Shakira.

"I do my best," Shakira replied. She nodded toward Moses.

"This is Moses Pritchard. The bike is for him."

Moses and Lee shook hands. She had a strong grip that matched her demeanor.

"Pleased to meet you. Heard you're from Newlanta."

"Yep."

"They say that's Paradise."

"They lied."

Lee laughed. She went to the bike and Moses followed.

"I tuned it up as much as I could. You should get a lot of miles out of it. I'm thinking at least five hundred before it needs more work."

"That's more than I need," Moses said.

"I replaced the storage units with extra fuel tanks to increase the range. The tanks are reinforced to resist gunfire. Thought that would be important for somebody like you."

"It is."

Moses sat on the bike. It was fairly comfortable, but that wasn't important. As long as it got him from A to B it would do."

"Thanks, Lee. Keys?"

Lee tossed him the keys.

"What about your dog?" Shakira asked.

"Frack will track me. I'll be moving too fast for it to keep up."

He stepped off the bike and gave Shakira a hug.

"Thanks for everything, killer," he said.

"Don't mention it," she replied. "Don't miss."

"I never do."

Moses started the bike, the shrill engine sound filling the shop. He nodded then sped out of the shed and onto the road out of Fox Valley. The gate guards waved him through with smiles, probably happy to see him and his troubles speed away. He rode to the peach groves before he stopped to study the map Shakira had given him. He was twenty miles from Jamal's main base; if the roads were good he should arrive in forty-five minutes. He folded the map then waited for Frack, picking a few peaches for his bag. The dog arrived ten minutes later.

Moses usually programmed Frack remotely, but he had a few commands for what was about to come that had to be entered manually. He switched the unit to shadow mode and retrieval. He didn't know what he was getting into, so he needed a way out if things got hot. It meant risking the dog, but it was a precaution he had to take. There was another he had to take as well.

Moses opened Frack's storage compartment then took out the manual radio. He flipped the switch; the green light indicated the batteries were still good. He pressed the button on the side then spoke into the microphone.

"Esmerelda?"

There was a brief silence.

"Moses. You in trouble already?"

"I stay in trouble. Hey, I need you to link with Frack...I mean MU Two."

"What happened to MU1?"

"Long story. I'm going into a hot situation and I don't know how long I'll be there."

"Or if you're coming out."

"Something like that. You might have to take over."

"Gotcha. You be safe out there."

"That's impossible."

A green light appeared on Frack's head unit. A few minutes later it blinked, indicating its link to Esmerelda. There were quite a few satellites still operating; for how much longer was anyone's guess. Rumor was a few of the Russian and Chinese territories were attempting to reach space again, but that was probably just wishful thinking. They'd suffered as much or more that everyone else. It was probably some warlord's boasting, claiming like most to return things to 'the way it used to be.' It was the way it used to be that almost killed the world.

The dirt bike was a good choice. Moses covered the smooth sections of highway quickly and handled the rough terrain with ease. He forgot how quiet the woods could be, not from lack of people, but from people hiding from the sound of an approaching vehicle. Nothing was safe until it's dead, his Pop used to say. Traveling in the open meant they were heavily armed or had friends nearby. On the other hand, traveling in the open made him vulnerable to an ambush. Moses was willing to take the chance. His brief encounter with Jamal gave him the sense that whatever was about to go down would happen soon.

The Highway 96 bridge that used to span Interstate 75 was still down. Moses eased the dirt bike down the steep embankment then zoomed across the open damaged roadway to the other side. As he emerged over the hill a shot rang out. The bullet hit his shoulder, spinning him off the dirt bike. Moses fell, hitting the round hard before rolling onto his back. To his relief his vest held but his shoulder hurt like hell. Instead of standing and searching for cover he lay still. He'd fallen behind the bike; whoever shot him would have to come close to finish him off.

Whoever shot him was coming fast. Moses eased his sidearms from their holsters as he listened to their footfalls crunch against the sandy soil.

"Let's make this quick!" one of them said.

Moses sat up and took aim. The interlopers froze in their tracks, their faces locked in surprise.

He was about to shoot when he saw the child. They were a family. The husband held a beat up 30-30 Winchester, the wife a 20 gauge shotgun most likely loaded with buckshot or slugs. The child held an ancient .38 special in her small dirty hands.

"Drop' em," Moses said.

Everyone dropped their guns except the child.

"Drop your gun, baby," the woman urged.

The child dropped the handgun then scurried to the woman's side.

"We're sorry," the man said, "But you know how it is."

Moses stood, his guns still trained on the family.

He took a good look at them. They were starving, of course. Most families were. He didn't care about the parents, it was the child that concerned him.

"Take the bike," he said. "Don't barter it. You'll be starving again in a few days by the looks of it."

The parents looked ashamed.

"If you ride down this highway for about twenty miles, you'll find a community that'll take you in. Don't go in with the bike. They gave it to me; if they see you on it, they'll think you killed me and they'll kill you. Understand?"

"Understood," the woman said. "Thank you."

"Don't thank me," Moses replied. "You haven't made it yet."

Moses kept his guns trained on them until they climbed onto the bike then sped away. He wasn't sure they would take his advice, but at least he gave them a chance. More than anyone did for his family.

He rubbed his aching shoulder as he began the trek to Jamal's compound. This part of the journey was familiar. He'd traveled this stretch of road for longer than he should have, fighting for a warlord that didn't deserve his skills. But he was a different person then, a callous, selfish, angry person. It was the Statesboro Raid that turned him. That was his low point. As soon as they returned to Robbins he took off. By the time he arrived at Newlanta he was done. No more fighting; no more killing. He kept his promise for two years. That's when Voorhees and the others discovered who he was. Now he was fighting for a different reason, or at least that's what he told himself. As Newlanta grew and prospered, he began having mixed feelings about its purpose.

He came across scattered settlements as he neared Robbins. Most were single shanties occupied by wary people. Some fled into their meager protection upon seeing him; others stood defiant with old weapons pointed at him. A few waved with smiles, probably assuming by his armed appearance that he served Jamal. He smiled and waved at all of them, hoping to avoid a firefight before he reached the city. The smell told him all he needed to know about the conditions. He figured if Jamal was serious about creating better conditions, he would have at least worked on improving the conditions of the squatters.

"Same old Jamal," he whispered.

Dusk crept across the landscape from the east but Moses kept walking. He had no intentions of bunking among squatters because that meant sleeping with one eye open and he was too tired. Instead he took out his infrared glasses and continued until he reached the outskirts of Robbins. The hostel he remembered from years ago was still there, with the addition of a sputtering neon sign. Talk about confidence in the system, he thought.

He took off the glasses as he neared the entrance. Two guards straightened when they saw him, both looking at each other nervously.

"Calm down," Moses said. "I'm just looking for a place to sleep for the night."

One of the guards, a young man with a pasty face and a staccato beard stepped toward him.

"We're going to have to take those guns," he said, his voice cracking.

"That's not going to happen," Moses replied. "Let's make a deal. I keep my guns and you stay alive."

The man took a step toward Moses. Moses snatched his Sigs free; the on in his right hand pressed into the man's chest, the other he pointed at the other guard. The man swallowed then stepped away. The other guard, a tall reddish woman wearing a dingy cap, cut him a mean glance.

"Keep'em," the guard said. "I don't get paid enough for this shit."

Moses turned toward the woman.

"Well?" he asked.

The woman hesitated then motioned for him to go inside.

Moses stepped through the door, guns still in his hands. The attendant at the desk jumped and immediately raised her hands.

"We don't have any credits!" she shouted.

"Put your hands down," Moses said as he put his guns away. "I'm here for a bunk. You got any rooms available?"

The woman eased her hands to her hips.

"How'd you get in here with those?" she asked.

"You need to hire braver help," Moses replied.

"Tell me about it," the woman said. She opened an index card box, shuffling through it with quick fingers. She took out a card with a key attached to it.

"Here you go. Room 12. It's got clean sheets and a working bathroom. There should be a pitcher of water on the night stand."

"How long has the water been there?" Moses asked.

"How am I supposed to know?" the woman replied. "I'm not housekeeping."

Moses took a quick scan of the lobby. "I don't think anybody is."

Moses took the key then trudged down the dimly lit hallway to his room. The last thing he was concerned about was shitty room service. A bed and a door he could lock was all he needed. He unlocked the door and entered the room. It was sparse but tolerable, the bedsheets paper thin but he didn't need them anyway. The water pitcher was empty. He sat his gear in the closet space then pushed the chair against the door to secure it. Moses place his guns strategically around the room before stripping down to his underwear and collapsing on the bed. He'd take a shower in the morning; there was only him to deal with his road funk, and he was used to it.

He slept hard that night, his dreams coming in confusing glimpses. He woke up in a start, springing upright and grabbing his Sig from the nightstand. The room was empty except for him. He tried to remember what sparked him to do so, but the dream slipped away like water between his fingers. It was probably best; most of his dreams were of bad experiences from his past. He stumbled to the bathroom. To his delight the shower worked. He took a quick shower with the ragged washcloth and used soap then went back into the room to dress. He was almost done when there was a knock on the door.

"What?" he shouted.

"Breakfast!" a woman answered.

Moses picked up the Sig. "I didn't ask for it."

"It comes with the room," the woman replied. "I can leave it at the door if you want."

Moses tucked his gun behind his back in his pants then moved the chair away from the door. When he opened it the woman from the lobby stood before him with a tray of peaches, scrambled eggs and grits. The clothes she barely fit suggested she was there for more than breakfast.

Moses took the tray.

"This is all I'm interested in. You got enough of my money."

He closed the door.

"Fucker!" she said.

"Not this morning," Moses replied.

He ate quickly then gathered his gear. He didn't bother stopping by the desk on his way out. It was hot and hazy outside, summer taking its last swipe before giving way to the fall. People were already about their daily routines, the road filled with walkers and riders in various forms of transportation. Moses headed for the city, thankful for the early breakfast. He reached the main gate for Robbins two hours later. There had been major improvements since his last visit; the barbed wire gate surrounding the city had been replaced with a stone perimeter. While not as impressive as Newlanta's, it was a sign that Jamal had acquired better resources. The guards at the gates lost their relaxed postures as they noticed him, their guns shifted in his direction. Moses raised his hands as he approached, a smile on his grizzled face.

The guard closest to him aimed his AR-15 at Moses.

"Who are you, killer?" he asked.

"Moses Pritchard. Watkins is expecting me."

The man lowered his gun. "Is he, now?"

"Call him," Moses replied.

"Why should we?" another guard asked.

"Because I asked you nice," Moses said.

"Jimmy, call base," the lead guard said, never taking his eyes or gun off Moses.

The guard closest to the gate raised a comm to his ear.

"Pete? We got a killer at the gate saying Commander Watkins invited him. Name is Moses Pritchard."

The seconds passed like minutes as they waited for the response. Moses figured he could take them all out, but not without taking a round or two. He cleared his head; he wasn't here to fight yet.

Jimmy's eyebrows rose.

"For real? Okay. Thanks Pete."

Jimmy placed the comm down. "He's legit. The commander said send him through. Asked me to escort him."

The lead guard seemed disappointed as he lowered his gun.

"Welcome to Robbins," he said.

He reached for Moses's weapons.

"No," Jimmy said. "The commander said let him through as is."

Moses saluted the guards as he followed Jimmy inside.

The roads of Robbins had improved since Moses fled, as had everything else. Probably the result of slave labor. This was the best restoration he'd seen outside Newlanta, which made him uncomfortable. Both cities were making great progress, yet both were close to coming to conflict with each other. It was times like this Moses wished he had skills with words. They didn't need a war. They needed to connect.

"So you must be some killer," Jimmy said.

Jimmy's words brought Moses back to reality.

"I guess I am," he replied.

"Moses Pritchard," Jimmy said. "Yeah, I've heard talk of you. A real badass. You took Statesboro practically by yourself."

Moses didn't answer. He wasn't proud of Statesboro.

"That was you, wasn't it?"

"How far before we get to Jamal's hideout?" Moses said.

"We got a ways to go," Jimmy said. "Hold up."

Jimmy got on the comm.

"Hey, how about sending a transport or something," he said. "I got precious cargo here."

He lowered the comm as he smiled.

"Our ride is on the way," he said. "I'm beginning to like hanging out with you."

"Don't get used to it," Moses said.

Jimmy laughed. "I won't."

Ten minutes later an armored Humvee rumbled up to them. The front passenger door swung open and a young guard trotted around the vehicle to open the rear passenger door.

"Get it," she said.

Jimmy and Moses climbed inside. Someone tried to make the refurbished seats comfortable and failed. They jostled over the pitted streets to the compound Moses thought he'd never see again. Nothing much had changed on the exterior except for a flagpole that flew a black flag with an embroidered leopard. Moses fought back a sigh; apparently Jamal was beginning to take himself seriously.

The Humvee pulled up to the entrance and the young guard opened their door.

"Welcome home, Gunman Pritchard," the guard said. "It's good to have you back on board."

Moses looked at the woman. She was too young to remember his time in Robbins; she probably wasn't even born yet. Someone had been talking about him, and that wasn't a good thing.

"Yeah," he replied.

"I'll take you . . ."

"That's okay," Moses said. "The place hasn't changed that much. I know the way."

Moses sauntered across the wide courtyard to the compound building, noting the watch towers and soldiers in various forms of training. Jamal was preparing to make a major move, another confirmation that Voorhees intelligence info was accurate. It was also the reason Jamal didn't try to kill him. If he was about to start a fight, he needed experienced gunmen. Jamal was a practical man; he'd sideline a grudge out of necessity. The question was what would he do once he got what he wanted.

When they reached Jamal's office the guards opened the door and stepped aside. A blast of cool air met them and Moses smiled; Jamal had rediscovered air conditioning. The man at the desk stood then extended his hand with a smile on his face. He wore military fatigues and new boots.

"Welcome Mr. Pritchard," the man said. "I'm Sergeant Percy Smothers. It's a pleasure to meet you."

"Likewise," Moses said. "Where's Jamal?"

"Commander Watkins is waiting for you in his office," Smothers said. Moses noticed he put an emphasis on commander. Apparently, he expected Moses to address Jamal the same way. That wasn't going to happen.

Smothers led him to Jamal's office. Like the courtyard, the office was busy, workers moving about with written orders and having intense conversations. Moses was getting the feeling he'd arrived too late. He needed to start planning his getaway.

Smothers led them to the door to Jamal's office. He knocked on the door.

"Who is it?" Jamal called out.

"Sir? Gunman Pritchard is here."

"Come in."

Smothers opened the door and Moses entered. Jamal sat behind a large oak desk, the surface covered with organized stacks of papers. He looked up at Moses and smiled.

"I didn't think you would come," he said.

"I was invited," Moses replied.

Jamal looked over his shoulder to Jimmy and Smothers.

"That will be all," he said.

"Yes sir!" the men said in unison.

Jamal motioned to the chair before his desk and Moses sat.

"Sir? Really? What's going on around here, Jamal?"

"Commander Watkins," Jamal corrected him.

"Hah," Moses said. "If you think I'm going to call you that you might as well kick me out of here now."

Jamal laughed. "I had to try."

Jamal opened the cigar box on his desk. "Smoke?"

Moses shook his head. "This isn't a friendly visit yet. I'm trying to figure out what you want from me that's so important that you didn't try to kill me."

"That's Moses," Jamal said. "Always straight to the point. To be honest that was my first instinct. But you had the drop on me. I thought about having you popped on your way to the base, but that would cost too many men and I can't afford to waste any right now."

"So, what's going on and why do you need me?"

Jamal took a cigar from the box.

"A lot has changed since you left," he said. "As you can see, we're no longer a glorified gang. It took me a while, but the results have been worth it."

"Why all the activity?"

"All any of us have wanted since The Collapse is peace," Jamal said.

Moses eyebrows rose. "Really? You could have fooled me."

"Those were the early days," Jamal replied. "It was brutal but necessary. And it's not like you don't have blood on your hands."

Moses didn't reply. Jamal clipped the end of his cigar then lit it.

"Here's the deal. I've pacified most of central Georgia, from Forsyth down to Tifton. We've got alliances west to Geneva, and we're negotiating with Savannah on the coast."

"And how were you able to work all that out?" Moses asked. "From what I remember you were not the best negotiator."

Jamal grinned. "I have a big stick. You remember the old military base, right?"

Moses stiffened. "Yeah."

"Guess who cracked the code?"

Moses sat up. "Bullshit."

"Real shit," Jamal replied. "Hacked it six years ago. Talk about the motherlode! Small arms, long rifles, explosives, armored cars, the whole shebang."

Moses did his best not to show his fear. With that kind of arsenal Jamal would be unstoppable.

"And that's not the best part," he continued. "We found another section of the base that was sealed off. Took us three years to crack that code, but we did."

"And what did you find?" Moses asked.

Jamal puffed the cigar then smirked.

"I'll show you."

Jamal stood then strolled to the door. Moses followed him into the office; Jimmy and the other guard fell in step with them. The Humvee waited outside. The guards opened the rear doors then Jimmy and the guard sat in front with the driver.

"Take us to the base," Jamal ordered.

The driver looked into the rearview mirror then saluted. He maneuvered the Humvee through the camp traffic to the main road. Moses peered through the small window, observing Robbins as they traveled to the base. The city, like most cities, was still recovering. Small homes nested among tents, tendrils of smoke from campfires rising into the hazy late summer sky. Everywhere people bustled about. They passed a number of open markets, a sign of prosperity. Still, it unnerved Moses to see so many soldiers about. Whatever was going on was not happening by consent. He knew Jamal. He was not the type of man skilled in patient debate and he was not used to being challenged.

The city clutter gave way to an empty expanse, a security buffer between the city and the old base. As they neared it Moses noted that the damaged fence had been replaced with a concrete wall. The entrance was heavily guarded. The driver blew his horn in a distinct cadence and the guards went into action, clearing the entrance and opening the gate. The Humvee entered unobstructed.

"We found the new section by chance," Jamal said. "We were searching for fuel near the airbase when one of the workers found the entrance. It was locked electronically so there was no way we could enter without the code."

"What happened to the worker that found the crypt?" Moses asked.

"He's dead," Jamal said. "Can't have secrets like this getting out, can we?"

"Guess not," Moses replied.

"Anyway, we thought we had no way to get in," Jamal continued. "Didn't want to try to blast it. Might screw up the electronics and never get in. We had to pick that lock."

"I know you didn't do it," Moses said. "You're not smart like that."

"Moses and his insults," Jamal commented. "I missed that about you. But yeah, I'm not smart like that. But we found someone that was, thanks to you."

Moses frowned. He knew what was coming next.

"Seems that one of the Statesboro refugees has a gift for such things."

They came upon the airfield. Workers were everywhere, repairing the old tarmac and clearing foliage. There were a few aircraft on the grounds with teams of workers swarming them like ants. Four hangars stood at the end of the tarmac. The more Moses saw, the more concerned he became.

The Humvee rolled into one of the hangers. Vehicles of all kinds were on display; armored Humvees, personnel carriers and some Moses didn't recognize.

"So what's better than this?" Moses asked.

"You'll see. We're almost there."

They passed through the central hanger and crossed another open expanse. At the end of the road was a small white building. The Humvee pulled up then stopped. Jamal and Moses waited for their doors to open then stepped outside. The building was heavily guarded; a squad of armed men and two operational tanks.

"You know, if I was looking for something important, I would come to this building," Moses commented. "All this security is obvious."

"I got nothing to worry about," Jamal said. "Or do I?"

Moses raised his hands. "Not from me."

One of the guards opened the door and they stepped into a long hallway with empty rooms on both sides Moses surmised that this was probably a building used for teaching or training. At the opposite end of the hallway was a staircase. Moses followed Jamal and the others down the spiraling stairs until they reached the bottom. Another long concrete hallway extended before them; as they walked Moses noticed the doors. He peeked into one of the rooms; it was filled with what looked like computer consoles and chairs.

"What is this?" Moses asked. "Some kind of command center?"

"Yes," Jamal said.

"Command for what?"

Jamal didn't answer. They reached the double doors at the end of the hallway.

"Prepare to be amazed," Jamal said.

He took out a key then opened the doors. They entered an underground hanger filled with aircraft like Moses had never seen before. They resembled conventional aircraft except there were no cockpits.

"What is this?" he asked.

"These are drone ships," Jamal said. "The rooms we passed are for the remote pilots."

Moses eyes went wide.

"I'll be damned," he said.

Jamal smiled. "I thought you would like this."

Moses walked through the room in awe. Newlanta was in deep trouble.

The massive storage room contained dozens of drone flying crafts and a few ground vehicles.

"It's not so much the equipment," Jamal said. "It's the technology. We know how to use it, we're just trying to figure out how to duplicate the technology. We have to adapt it to what we have available, which isn't much."

Moses didn't reply. He sized up the arsenal, trying to figure out what Newlanta had that could thwart such an onslaught.

"So, what do you think, killer?" Jamal asked.

"I think somebody's in some deep shit," Moses replied.

Jamal laughed. "Me, too. I think I can control the south in nine months, maybe a year. After things settle, I can shift north and deal with Newlanta."

"Sounds like a plan," Moses replied. "What do I have to do with all this?"

"I was waiting for you to ask."

Jamal took his unfinished cigar from his vest.

"Truth is I should have killed your ass the moment I knew you were back. Fuck Fox Valley and everything else. You hurt me, Moses."

"I wasn't your girlfriend," Moses said. "I just worked for you."

"I trusted you, bitch!" Jamal said, pointing at Moses with his cigar. "And my trust doesn't come easy."

"Just what the fuck did I do?" Moses retorted. "Did anybody come down here and take your shit? No. I just left, Jamal. I was tired of this shit. I was tired of your shit."

"But now you're back," Jamal said.

"Yeah, I'm back."

Jamal lit his cigar, taking a few puffs before speaking.

"Why?"

"I told you. I got bored."

Jamal stopped walking. The guards flanked him, hands on their guns.

"You sure Voorhees didn't send you to spy on me?"

Moses sighed. "The last thing Voorhees wants is a fight. All he wants is his utopia. Now he'll put up a scrap if you come after him, but he's not going to start one. Leave him alone and he'll leave you alone."

Jamal was silent, puffing his cigar as he stared at Moses. Moses stared back. This wasn't good odds. He was sure he could take all three of them, but not without a few wounds. Then he would have to fight his way off the base. Now that would be a problem, depending on how Jamal's little army responded to his demise.

"Still, I should have killed you," Jamal said. "But I'm a practical man. Not many people in or out of the Wild have your skills. I need people like you."

"You got me, if the price is right."

"Oh, the price is right. Twenty percent over what I paid you before. A house within the compound with running water and electricity."

"So far, so good," Moses replied.

"Plus rank," Jamal said. "You'll command my southern forces."

"Wait just a minute," Moses said. "I'm a gunman. I'm no leader. I can't be responsible for a bunch of asshats."

"You underestimate yourself," Jamal said. "You can't forget about Statesboro. That was some beautiful work."

Jamal was right. He couldn't forget about Statesboro, no matter how hard he tried. Moses didn't want to take the command, but he was in Robbins to find out as much as he could about Jamal's operation then take him out. What better way than being part of the chain of command?"

"If I agree," Moses said. "I report only to you, nobody else."

"I wouldn't have it any other way," Jamal replied. "That way I can keep my eye on you. You're not in the clear yet."

"That's fair," Moses replied.

Jamal took another puff.

"It's settled then. Let's get back to the office. I'll have the guards take you to your new home. Jimmy, you're assigned to Moses. You do whatever he tells you to."

"Yes sir," Jimmy replied.

"I don't need an assistant," Moses said.

"That's not your choice," Jamal replied. "I said I was going to keep an eye on you. I meant it."

Moses looked at Jimmy and Jimmy grinned.

"Perfect," he said.

They left the drone compound and loaded up in the Humvee.

"Take us to Sector Four," Jamal told the driver.

Sector Four was the south side of the city. It was a smaller version of Jamal's sector, with soldiers going about their daily routine and training. The Humvee pulled up to the compound office and everyone exited. Jamal led the way through the door. The office staff stood and saluted.

"Okay everyone, I'd like to introduce you to your new commander, Moses Pritchard."

The staffers saluted Moses. He could tell by their expressions that they were not happy.

"Sir," one of the staffers said. "What about Commander Edwards?"

"He's been reassigned," Jamal said. "If anyone has an issue with the change let me know now.

I don't need any problems; if you can't adjust, you'll be reassigned."

No one responded, as Moses expected. The word 'reassigned' could mean many things to Jamal, none of them good.

"Excellent!" Jamal said. He turned to Moses.

"I'll leave you to get acquainted with your new job. I need to see you tomorrow at six a.m. sharp. We have work to do."

"You don't waste time, do you?" Moses said.

"You know me, killer. See you tomorrow."

Jamal and the others left the office. The staffer that asked about Commander Edwards walked up to him then took off her glasses.

"Commander Edwards is a good man," she said. "His shoes will be hard to fill."

"I'm not trying to fill his shoes," Moses replied. "I'm here to do a job. Which way to the office?"

The woman put on her glasses. "This way . . .sir."

The staffer took him to Edwards's former office. It was a mess. Maps were strewn across the desk and file drawers overflowed. Moses looked at the staffer skeptically and she shrugged.

"Commander Edwards wasn't very organized," she said. "But he had amazing intuition."

"I bet," Moses replied. "What's your name?"

"Shalonda. Shalonda Keys."

"What's your rank?"

"Sergeant."

"Well, Sergeant Keys, your first assignment is to help me get this office organized. Jimmy?"

"Yes sir!"

"Does this place have any coffee?"

"Yes, sir."

"Excellent. Bring me a couple of pots. It's going to be a long night."

Moses and Jimmy worked on the pile on the desk, separating them by subject matter. Keys returned a few minutes later with the coffee then went to work on the file cabinet. Keys stopped organizing the drawers to stare at Moses.

"Is it true what they say about Statesboro?" she asked.

Moses stopped working on the papers and dropped his head.

"It depends on what you heard," he replied.

"Everybody talks about it like it was some kind of genius campaign. I've studied it. It was some cruel shit."

"It was both," Moses said.

"All those people," she said.

"I didn't ask you to help me to discuss the past," he said.

"Yes, sir," Keys replied.

The office was organized after another three hours. Moses dismissed Jimmy. He sat down then began studying the maps.

"This plan sucks," he said.

Keys looked over his shoulder.

"Why do you say that?"

"Because it's not a plan," he replied.

"That's how Edwards worked. He devised the plan as the attack progressed."

"I bet a lot of folks died while he improvised."

"And you have a problem with that?"

Moses slammed his palm on the desk.

"Look Keys, I see you have a problem with me. Now you and I both know that we're stuck with each other. Just do what I need you to do without

the comments and we'll get along fine. Keep this
shit up and I'll ask for you to be reassigned."

Keys glared at him and Moses nodded.

"Take your frustration out on your partner if
you have one. Right now, we need to work."

Keys nodded then sat. Moses looked at the
maps again. South Georgia was controlled by three
separate factions united for one reason; to oppose
Jamal. Two of the factions; the Southern Knights
and the Dixie Boys, were white supremist groups.
Moses scowled; some people didn't know how to let
go of the past. The other, the Freedom Fighters, was
an amalgamation of people opposed to everything
the Dixie Boys and Southern Knights stood for. The
fact that they had come together to oppose Jamal
didn't say much for their current leadership.

"Divide and conquer," Moses said.

Keys looked at him. "What?"

Moses stood. Come on, let's go talk to
Jamal."

"He said you had till tomorrow."

"I don't need that much time."

Moses marched out of the office with Keys
trailing behind. Jimmy stood then opened the door
for them.

"Get us a ride Jimmy," Moses ordered.

"Back in a few," Jimmy replied.

Jimmy returned with a cargo truck. Moses
and Keys climbed in and they traveled to Jamal's
compound. Jamal was surprised to see them.

"Trouble already?" he said.

"Nope," Moses said. He spread out the map
on Jamal's desk.

"The Freedom Fighters are the weak link," he
said. "They're only in this alliance because they're
scared of you. Send them a peace offering. Let them

know that no harm will come to them and they get to keep control of their territory."

Jamal looked at the map. "It would be a lie."

"That doesn't matter," Moses replied. "They have the largest force. All we need them to do is sit on the sidelines while we deal with the Knights and the Boys. If we're lucky they might join in."

"Or we can stick to Edwards's plan," Jamal said.

"That's up to you," Moses replied. "If you want me to lead my troops down there I will. But you're going to lose a lot of them in the process. These are fighters. They're going to make you pay for every inch of ground, which is going to delay your move on Newlanta for at least a year."

"I'm not in a hurry," Jamal said.

"You should be," Moses replied.

"What do you know that you're not sharing?" Jamal asked.

"Newlanta isn't aggressive," Moses said. "But every day it gets stronger. We can go play around with these rednecks to secure our rear, but we need to be quick about it."

Jamal smiled. "See, I knew you were a leader."

"Nope, I'm just practical. So what are we going to do?"

"Send a person to the Fighters. Cut a deal with them. I'll let you sort out the details."

"I'm not sending anyone," Moses said. "I'm going."

"No," Jamal said. "I need you here."

"For what? You got the plan. If I don't come back you can send someone else. Besides, I can be more persuasive."

Jamal leaned back in his chair. "You do have a reputation."

Moses nodded.

"Go," Jamal said. "But take Jimmy and Keys with you. I'll make Edwards interim commander until you return."

"He's still alive?" Moses said.

Jamal laughed. "I'm not as bad as you remember."

Moses and the others returned to their camp. He spent the rest of the day studying the maps and planning a route to the Freedom Fighters territory. It was dark when Jimmy poked his head into the office.

"Sir, isn't about time for you to call it a day?"

Moses looked through the blinds into the darkness.

"Probably so. Any idea where I'm bunking?"

Jimmy smiled. "Yep."

Jimmy took him to the officers' quarters, a section of the camp occupied by shipping crates converted into homes. Jimmy gave him the key.

"See you tomorrow, commander," Jimmy said.

Moses waved as he entered his crate home. It was modest but functional. He dropped his gear then laid on the bed catching a little rest and making sure the area was settled before taking the controller from his pack and summoning Frack. He went outside and waited; moments later Frack trotted up to him. He put on his communicator and buzzed Esmerelda.

"Jeez Moses, don't you sleep?"

Moses laughed. "You go to bed too early."

"I have a real job, remember. Killing people is easier."

"You should do it more often," Moses said. "Hey, check this out."

Moses sent the images captured by Frack then described everything he'd seen in detail.

"Oh my God!" Esmerelda said. "We're in trouble. I have to share this with Voorhees."

"Not yet," Moses said. "Voorhees sees this and he'll attack Jamal yesterday. That's what I'm trying to avoid."

"What's your move?"

"Jamal made me a commander," Moses explained. "He's given me an assignment to prove myself."

"It doesn't have anything to do with Newlanta, does it?"

"Not directly, but he does have his sights on Newlanta and he's not interested in negotiating."

"He doesn't have to with those drones," Esmerelda replied.

"Is it that bad?"

"Depends. If the drones are equipped with conventional firepower, we can probably hold our own. We have our own secrets."

The statement caused Moses to raise his eyebrows.

"What do you mean, 'our own secrets'?"

"That's on a need to know basis, and you don't need to know," Esmerelda replied.

"I don't like operating in the dark," Moses said.

"You're going to have to. I told you too much already. Anyway, from what I read some of those old tech drones were armed with lasers. If they are, we've got issues."

"Lasers?" Moses said. "Sounds dangerous."

"They are," Esmerelda said.

"How can you know for sure?"

"I need images. Can you get them?"

"I'm not sure. Jamal might get suspicious if I ask to go there again. I'll have to work it out after we secure South Georgia. He should have more confidence in me then."

"Good."

"One more thing," Moses said.

"What?"

"I'm going to have to give him something about Newlanta. What do you have?"

"I don't know, Moses."

"Come on Esmerelda. I need something that looks more important that it is."

"Get back with me when you return from down south. I might have something."

"Good. And don't talk to Voorhees. At least not yet."

"Gotcha."

Moses broke contact, then sent Frack away. He went inside then sat at his desk studying the maps until fatigue forced him to sleep. It wasn't restful. Images of Statesboro flashed in his head the entire night, waking him several times. He finally succumbed to the nightmares, going into his pack and taking one of his pills. There were only three remaining; he'd have to scope out some wrecked pharmacy locations to hunt out more. He didn't know how long it would take him to get back to Newlanta, so he didn't have the luxury to wait. He took the pill then laid back on his pillow. Sleep came moments later.

- 5 -

Moses was groggy from the medicine when he woke. He dressed slowly then washed up the best he could. He'd forgotten to ask where the mess was located, so it took him a few minutes to find it. As he entered the soldiers stood at attention. Moses smirked. These bitches were serious about playing army.

"At ease," he said.

The soldiers sat and continued their meals. He was heading to the line when he saw Jimmy sitting a table separated from the rest of the troops. Keys sat with him. Jimmy waved him over.

"Morning," he said.

"Good morning, sir," Jimmy replied. Keys said nothing.

Moses sat, his eyes on Keys.

"What are you doing here?" he asked.

"Jamal contacted me last night," she replied. "I'm going with you."

"Jimmy's not enough?"

"Jimmy likes you. I don't." Keys said.

Moses laughed. "Let's get in line."

"No sir," Jimmy said. "The staff will bring you your breakfast."

"I'm beginning to like this place more and more every day."

The cooks brought them grits, eggs and bacon and coffee. Moses ate the breakfast but skipped the coffee. He never had need of it, and the one time he drank it his nightmares were worse. After breakfast Jimmy secured a Humvee for them. Moses laid the map on the hood.

"I mapped out a route for us. It's going to take longer than if we stayed close to the highway, but we'll avoid quite a few obvious ambush points."

"That's a lot of off road," Jimmy said. "I'm not sure this baby can take it."

"We'll push it as long as we can. If it breaks down, we'll walk."

Keys looked at the map. "What about ferals?"

"What about them?" Moses asked.

"You're taking us through some thick Wild. We're bound to run into a few."

"Then we'll deal with them as they come."

"It won't be that easy," Keys said.

Moses ignored his urge to curse Keys out.

"If you haven't noticed, I'm not new to this," he said. "I've spent a good part of my life roaming this shit alone. You could even say I've been a feral myself. If I'm not worried about them, you shouldn't be."

"My situation is different," Keys said.

Moses finally realized what Keys was referring to.

"Like you or not, you're with me," he said. "You don't have anything to worry about."

Keys frowned. There was nothing Moses could do to dissuade her for now. He folded the map.

"Let's go," he said.

They loaded their gear and set out for the south. Moses decided to leave most of his guns at the base. He was acting as a commander and showing up fully packed would send the wrong message. He settled for his Sigs, the HK MP5 and his Winchester Model 70 sniper rifle. They were sturdy weapons and rounds were common and easy to scavenge. Jimmy and Keys were armed with AR-15s and G17 Glock 9mms. Jimmy also carried a sawed off 12-gauge shotgun.

The drive to I-95 took them a full day. It would have been much shorter using I-16, but Moses wanted to avoid contact as much as possible. They were forced to break protocol just beyond old Dublin due to the swamps and creeks, but luckily the area was sparsely populated. Moses felt nervous as they approached the Statesboro exit; old memories surfaced.

"Just like old times," Keys commented.

"Shut the fuck up," Moses replied.

Keys grinned. "Don't know why you're pissed off. This was your shining moment."

"I did what I had to do," Moses replied. "Nothing shining about killing people."

"Especially when most of them are innocent," Keys said.

"What world do you live in?" Moses asked. "Everybody in this vehicle has blood on their hands."

"Some more than others," Keys snapped.

She wasn't going to stop, Moses realized. It took him a minute to figure out way.

"You're a survivor," he said.

Keys didn't reply.

"I guess I didn't get everybody."

It was a low blow, so he was waiting when Keys spun in his direction, her Glock in her hand. He grabbed the weapon in a chamber lock then slammed her head against the roof. He twisted in his seat, elbowing her across the jaw.

"What the hell?" Jimmy shouted.

"Stop the car!" Moses ordered.

He pulled the Glock from Keys stunned hands, then reached across to open her door. He shoved her out with his foot. Keys landed hard just at the Humvee came to a stop, striking her head on the pavement. Moses stepped out of the vehicle then squatted beside her.

"What the hell were you thinking? You think you can do this yourself? You think Jamal would let you slide?"

"Fuck you and Jamal!" Keys said. She held her head where it hit the pavement, tears in her eyes.

"My family died in Statesboro. You killed them all!"

Moses shut his eyes tight for a moment, pushing back the memories.

"Things got out of hand," he said. "Once it began, I couldn't stop it."

"You didn't have to come," Keys said. "We weren't a threat to anyone. We were just trying to survive like everyone else."

"Everyone's a threat to Jamal," Moses said. "Why do you think we're heading south? Besides, I was a different man then."

Keys glared at him. "Really? So why are you back?"

"I got my reasons."

Moses stood then extended his hand.

"You got a choice. You can come with us or you can stay here. We still have a mission to complete."

"You're not going to kill me?" Keys asked.

"Why? If I were you, I would have tried the same thing. You'll have to promise me you won't try it again. I won't believe you, but I'll take my chances."

Keys grabbed his hand. As he was pulling her up, she went for her knife. Moses sidestepped her thrust then punched her across the jaw. She fell again, this time unconscious.

Jimmy stood beside him.

"Did she get you?"

Moses inspected himself. The blade sliced his shirt and scratched his skin.

"Almost."

Jimmy took out his Glock and took aim.

"No," Moses said. He reached down, lifted Keys onto his shoulder and carried her to the nearest cover. He placed her down in the brush.

"We're just going to leave her here?" Jimmy asked.

"Bring her gear," he told Jimmy.

They placed the gear beside her with a few days' worth of rations.

"Better here alive than here dead," Moses answered. "Let's go."

They climbed into the Humvee and continued their journey. After a few minutes of silence Jimmy spoke.

"You're not like I expected you to be," he said.

"What did you expect?" Moses asked.

"I thought you'd be . . . tougher."

Moses laughed. "Depends on the situation."

"I heard you were a real bad ass. I'm mean, burn it all down type of brother. And here you are giving folks second chances and shit. The Moses Pritchard I heard about would have killed Keys without a second thought."

"Sometimes folks deserve second chances."

Jimmy sucked his teeth. "I ain't met one yet."

"Why are you following Jamal?" Moses asked Jimmy. "What's in it for you?"

"Security," Jimmy said without hesitation. "You know how it is. It ain't called the Wild for nothing. It was either spend every day waiting for someone to sneak up on me and slit my throat or fall in with people that will keep me safe."

"Yeah, it's all about being safe," Moses said. "It's interesting what we'll give up to feel that way."

"What do you mean?" Jimmy asked.

"Nothing," Moses replied.

They drove the rest of the day in silence. By nightfall they were a few miles outside of Savannah. Jimmy found a good area to hide the Humvee and set up camp. Since they were unfamiliar with the area, they ate cold rations and took turns on watch during the night. Moses was awake when the sun rose over the slash pines and live oaks. He woke Jimmy and they ate a quick breakfast before setting out.

Two hours later they reached the I-16/I-95 junction.

"Pull over," Moses said.

Jimmy pulled to the side of the dilapidated road.

"What's up?" he asked.

"You don't hear it?" Moses asked.

"Hear what?"

Moses frowned. "Firefight."

He jumped from the Humvee.

"Hide it."

Jimmy drove the vehicle heavy brush. Moses climbed out of the vehicle with his HK. Jimmy shut off the Humvee and exited with his AR.

"You don't have to come," Moses said.

"I'm with you, killer," Jimmy said.

Moses nodded and they trotted into the woods. As they neared the junction the shooting was more obvious. They crouched as they reached a small rise; by the time they reached the summit they were crawling.

Moses peered through the trees to the scene below. It was a full out firefight, vehicles scattered in the highway, fighters crouched behind them trading shots.

"Merry Christmas," Moses whispered.

"What?" Jimmy asked.

"Couldn't have planned this better myself. Looks like a caravan of Freedom Fighters ran into toll collectors on their way back home."

Moses pointed out the Freedom Fighters to Jimmy, the fighters wearing their signature black berets.

"Who are the other fighters?"

"Don't know. Could be raiders, could be a new faction. Doesn't matter either way. The cavalry just arrived."

Moses unstrapped his long rifle then attached the scope and bipod. He loaded rounds then took his time sighting each fighter.

"Whoever I miss, you shoot," he said.

"I'll try," Jimmy said.

Moses checked his sighting one more time before taking a breath then letting it out slowly. As the last of the air left his lungs he fired. Four raiders were down before they realized they were being ambushed; another three were dead before they had sense enough to run for cover. Jimmy shot at the survivors as they fled for cover, taking down two more. Moses swung his rifle toward the Freedom Fighters. As he suspected they were looking in their direction, with guns aiming at them.

He placed down the rifle.

"Now comes the tricky part," he said. He took a white handkerchief from his bag then jammed his Sauer in his pants behind his back.

"I'm going out," he told Jimmy. "If I'm lucky we'll meet new friends. If I'm not, you'll have an interesting story to tell Jamal when you get back."

"If I get back," Jimmy said.

Moses winked at Jimmy then stepped into the open, waving the handkerchief. To his relief none of the Freedom Fighters shot him. He'd only taken a few steps before a Freedom Fighter yelled at him.

"That's close enough!"

"That's the way you say thank you?" Moses replied.

Three Freedom Fighters advanced on him. Moses waited as they approached. They searched him, frowning when they found his Sauer. Moses smiled.

"You never know," he said.

"Move," one of the fighters said.

Moses walked down the median hill to the Fighters. Their commander, a woman with a ragged scar across her forehead walked up to him, looking him up and down.

"I'm assuming you wanted to thank me up close and personal," Moses said.

"Who are you?" the woman asked in a husky voice. "And why did you help us?"

"Moses Pritchard," he answered. "I'm just a messenger."

"Bullshit," the woman replied. "You're a gunman."

"That too," Moses confessed.

"Who sent you?"

"Commander Jamal Watkins of Robbins," Moses said.

He saw the woman flinch. She turned then stalked away.

"Bring him. We're behind schedule."

The others prodded him to follow. He hated leaving his gear and Jimmy, but if things got tight he'd get more. Jimmy was on his own.

"Let's get moving!" the woman shouted. "We're late!"

The Fighters gathered their dead and wounded then loaded them into their trucks. Moses was pushed into the back seat of the commander's vehicle, the two guards sitting on either side of him. The vehicles lined up then sped down the highway.

The commander spoke to him.

"What the fuck does Watkins want with us?"

"A deal," Moses said.

"Bullshit," the commander replied.

"No shit," Moses countered. "You're playing with fire allied with the Knights and the Guard. "You got the good land and you're the wrong color."

"Like that makes a difference to Watkins."

"It doesn't," Moses agreed. "But he's coming whether you like it or not. It will go better for you if you're on the right side when he arrives."

"I think we'll be just fine."

"No you won't," Moses said. "Between you and me, Watkins just cracked the code on Robbins Air Force Base. He's got firepower you couldn't imagine. Trying to stop him now would be like taking a toothpick to a knife fight."

The commander was silent for a moment. "Why should I believe you?"

"Like you said, I'm a gunman. I was paid to deliver a message and I've seen what he has. But I'm guessing you're not the one who has the final say so I'll just wait until we get wherever we're going before I say anything else."

The commander turned in her seat. "Who says you're . . ."

Moses reached over the man to his left, opened his door then shoved him out of the vehicle. He punched the man to his right as he disarmed him then poked the commander in the forehead with the tip of the rifle barrel. He glared at the driver looking at him in the rear view mirror.

"Keep driving," he said.

The commander turned around.

"You heard him," she said.

They continued down I-95, the soldiers in the other vehicles unaware of the situation in their truck. Moses glanced out of the window as they traveled further south. Like most of the region, nature had reclaimed what was once farmland and towns. The appearance of ragged Rebel flags posted near the exit let him know they'd entered Southern Knights territory. Moses tightened his grip on the gun as they approached a Knight checkpoint; their vehicle slowed as they were waved through. The alliance was real, although there were no friendly exchanges between the caravan and the gatekeepers. The Knights were white supremacists; some people held on to old beliefs despite their destructive and divisive results.

The caravan exited off the main highway ten miles later. Like the highway, the two-lane thoroughfare was well-maintained. It seemed the entire region was coming back to life.

The wild brush gradually gave way to cultivated farmland. This was Freedom Fighter country. They were one of the oldest factions, created as a defense force after the Collapse. They were never aggressive; just a collective of farmers and others determined to protect their farms and families. Their alliance with the Knights was out of necessity. It was an uneasy peace bound to break sooner or later and Moses was there to make sure it happened sooner.

Vehicles separated from the caravan as the drivers and passengers reached their homes; soon Moses's vehicle was the only one on the road. The driver turned off on a dirt road, driving between fields that surpassed anything he'd seen in Fox Valley. Though the land in the Valley was more fertile, the Fighters were longtime farmers and knew how to get the best from the land. A cooperation between the two would yield amazing results, Moses mused. That was an idea for another time. First things first.

The truck took another turn down a one-way dirt road. They traveled through pastureland, the grazing cattle barely noticing their passing. At the end of the road was a large house surrounded by other buildings of various sizes. The door opened to the house and people emerged, most of them armed.

"Looks like someone called ahead," Moses said.

"What did you expect?" the commander said. "I don't think you can shoot your way out of this one, killer."

"I never planned to," Moses said. "I just wanted to make sure I got where I was going."

Moses extended the gun over the seat, giving it to the commander. She took the gun then looked at Moses in amazement. He grinned.

"Like I told you, I'm here to talk."

The truck pulled into the roundabout then stopped in front of the house. The commander and the others got out first. Moses stepped out, his hands raised. A man and woman in coveralls and wearing straw hats approached him. The armed ones moved closer, weapons ready.

The woman looked Moses up and down before speaking.

"Who we got here, Charlene?"

"He's a gunman working for Watkins," Charlene said. "His name is Moses Pritchard."

"I heard of him," the man said.

"I hoped someone would have," Moses replied.

"That don't mean shit," the man replied. "You ain't in the clear yet. Why are you here?"

"Watkins wants to parley," Moses said. "He's making a move this way and wants you on his side."

"We're good," the woman said. "You wasted his time and ours."

"Get him out of here," the man said.

The man and woman walked toward the house.

"You might want to hear the rest of what I have to say," Moses said.

"We don't."

"I'm not really here for Watkins," Moses continued. "I'm here on behalf of Newlanta."

The pair stopped then turned around.

"Commander Voorhees of Newlanta security sent me," Moses continued.

"Bring him inside," the woman said.

Moses followed the man and woman into the house. The sitting area was filled with refurbished furniture, some of it probably from before the Collapse. They passed through the room and entered the kitchen. The man and woman took a seat. They motioned for Moses to sit as well. The man extended his hand.

"Darrell Jones," he said.

Moses and the man shook. The woman sat back, her arms folded across her chest.

"Monica Jones," she said.

"Good to meet you," Moses said, thankful for old Southern traditions. "Husband and wife?"

They both laughed.

"Brother and sister," Monica said. "So why are you really here?"

"Voorhees heard Watkins might be planning to make a move against Newlanta. I volunteered to find out."

"So, you're working for Watkins to get some inside dirt," Darrell said.

Moses nodded. "And what I found out should have us all concerned."

"Why come to us?" Monica asked.

"Because I don't give a shit about the Knights for obvious reasons. Watkins knows your alliance with them is shaky at best. He wants y'all to sit on the sidelines when he decides to attack."

"What is he offering us?"

MILTON J DAVIS

"An equal alliance, but we all know that's bullshit."

Monica and Darrell nodded.

"I'm here to offer you a different deal," Moses said. "Ally with Newlanta. You can accept Watkin's deal and it will keep him off your back for the moment, but you know he'll eventually come for you. Join with Newlanta and you'll be protected. Once Newlanta deals with Watkins you'll be good to go."

"How is Newlanta going to 'deal' with them?" Monica asked.

"Commander Voorhees will try to negotiate first," Moses said. "If that doesn't work, things will get ugly, but not for long."

"How do you know?" Darrell nodded.

"If negotiations break down, I'll do what I was sent to do," Moses replied.

"And what is that?" Monica asked.

"Kill Watkins," Moses answered.

Monica and Darrell looked at each other before standing.

"You say you've been with Watkins for a while now. Why is he still alive?" Darrell asked.

"Because I'm not interested in being a martyr," Moses said. "Can't kill a man surrounded by his army. When I realized what he was planning, I decided to gather more information. But believe me, when the time comes, I'll take him out."

Monica and Darrell locked eyes as if in a telepathic conversation. Moses felt his fate was being decided. He hoped they would side with him; he would hate having to kill them. The siblings turned his way.

"Wait here," Monica said.

The brother and sister left Moses alone. He immediately began searching the kitchen for anything to protect himself. He was rummaging through the drawers by the sink when an elder voice stopped him.

"Ain't no need for you to do that," the woman said. "We ain't gonna hurt you, Moses."

Moses turned and was met by the smiling face of a dark-skinned gray-haired woman with a gently weathered face. She wore a simple green sundress covered with yellow daisies. She pulled out a chair then sat.

"Sit down and let me get a good look at you boy," she said. "Last time I saw you, you was a little baby."

"Saw me?" Moses sat at the table, overwhelmed by curiosity. "You know me?"

The woman nodded. "Sure do. I was good friends with your mama and daddy."

"My mama and daddy didn't have any friends," Moses replied.

"They did," she said. "At least before you were born. Terrence and Shanisha were always the quiet type, but once you came into the world, they got real private."

Moses stared at the woman in wonder. She knew his parents' names. It's possible she did some research, but where? He never told anyone.

"You say you knew my parents? How?"

"The four of us roamed together," the woman said. "Me, Horace, Terrence and your mama. Me and Shanisha were close. I never cared too much for your daddy, but they came as a pair so I had to tolerant him."

Moses smiled. His father could be a hard man to get along with. But he was gentle and loving to his family. It was a side anyone who met him never saw.

"So, what happened?" Moses said. "Why didn't my parents end up here?"

"They had a chance to," the woman said. "Word got out that some black folks were forming a faction down south. Back then Newlanta or any city was a hell hole. It was safer in the countryside. And white folks were being white folks, so a group of us headed south. We decided that if the rumors were true, we'd join. If they weren't, we'd make them true. We were tired of running and hiding."

The woman looked away as if recalling an earlier time.

"Shanisha was pregnant with you around then. She had you right before we were ready to move. Terrence was always difficult but after you were born, he got down right belligerent. Said he wasn't taking his family anywhere to be a sitting target. He believed the best way to stay safe was to keep moving. Shanisha did too, but I think if Terrence hadn't been so hard-headed I could have talked her into coming. Your life would have been a whole lot different if I had. Figure you wouldn't be roaming around killing folks."

Moses wasn't proud of what he did, but hearing the woman say it made him feel worse about it.

"I do what I have to do to survive," he said. "And it's worked out."

"I see," she said. "You have a lot of your daddy in you, but quite a bit of your mama too."

The woman got out of her seat, came over to Moses then hugged him. It was a warm, motherly hug that Moses immediately responded to. He hugged the woman tight as his eyes glistened.

"You smell like her," he said.

"Me and Shanisha were always partial to cocoa butter when we could find it," she said.

She let Moses go then shuffled back to her seat.

"We're going to let you work your deal," she said. "Tell Commander Watkins we're on his side and tell Voorhees the truth. No matter what happens we're fighting for what's ours."

"You can trust me ma'am," Moses said. "I won't let anything happen to you or your people."

"I know you won't," she said with a smile. "You're Shanisha's boy."

The woman turned to the door.

"Monica! Darrell! Y'all come back in here!"

The siblings came back into the kitchen.

"Give Moses back his things and anything else he needs. Make sure he gets through Knight territory safe."

"Yes, mama," they both said.

The woman stood.

"It was so good to see you, Moses."

Moses stood and she hugged him one more time.

"I'm Miss Darla, by the way."

"Thank you, Miss Darla," Moses said. "Thank you for bringing back my past."

"You should stay the night," Miss Darla said.

"I think I will."

"Darrell, take Moses to the guest house."

"Yes, ma'am."

"Do you have a watch, Moses?"

"Yes ma'am," Moses replied.

"Good. We eat supper at six. Don't be late. And wash your hands."

Moses laughed. "Yes ma'am."

"Follow me," Darrell said.

He led Moses out of the house to the barn. To Moses relief there were no animals inside, only ancient tractors in various stages of repair. A flight of stairs led to a small apartment on the second level.

"Supper's at six," Darrell said.

"Thank you," Moses replied.

"Don't thank me," Darrell replied. "If it was up to me you would be dead. But Mama's word is law. The man you pushed out the truck is a good friend of mine."

"I'm sorry," Moses said.

"No, you're not," Darrell replied. "You're lucky he didn't die. Damned lucky."

Moses climbed the stairs to the room. It was functional; a small bed with a nightstand and a chest of drawers. A writing desk sat opposite the bed. It was just the place for a mechanic working too late to crash out from exhaustion. Moses took off his clothes and slept until a knock on the door woke him.

"Yep?" he called out.

"Supper's ready," Monica said.

Moses dressed then descended to the lower level. Monica waited, her hands in her pockets as she whistled a familiar tune.

"My daddy used to whistle that same song," Moses said.

Monica looked at him and smiled.

"Apparently it was popular a long time ago."

"Do you know the words?" he asked.

"No, but Mama does. She sings bits and pieces of it but never the whole thing."

They walked to the main house together.

"Your brother wants to kill me," Moses said.

"Yeah. He and Troy are good friends."

"I take it you don't agree."

"Troy is an asshole," Monica said. "Despite that he doesn't deserve to die. At least not like that. But if he did, I wouldn't lose any sleep over it."

"So, I have two people on my side."

Monica stopped walking, giving Moses a cold stare.

"I'm not on your side," she said. "You're a stranger, and strangers have never brought anything good to us. Always begging and taking and never leaving anything behind. Mama knew your people, but she doesn't know you. We'll see if you're a person of your words."

"I'm not here to hurt anybody," Moses said. "I helped your crew on the road."

"And you pushed Troy out of the truck," Monica said. "You're a by-any-means-necessary brother."

"I'm practical," Moses replied.

"That's what I just said."

Monica continued walking.

"Come on. Supper's getting cold."

The kitchen smelled delicious. Miss Darla set the table as Darrell checked on the food simmering on the wood stove. He cut Moses a mean glance and he entered; Moses responded with a smile. Miss Darla inspected the table then nodded.

"Everybody join hands," she said.

A jolt of nostalgia struck Moses. He couldn't remember the last time he prayed. He grasped hands with Monica and Darrell. They held their mother's hands.

"Dear Lord, please bless us with the bounty we are about to receive. Bless the hands that prepared this meal, and share you traveling grace with those of us who are about to partake a perilous journey. In Jesus's name we pray. Amen."

"Amen," they said in unison.

Darrell pulled Miss Darla's chair from the table and she sat. Moses did the same for Monica. She smiled.

"Thank you," she said.

Moses winked.

Moses sat down to a plate of brown rice, fried chicken, collard greens and cornbread. He was eating better than he'd had in quite some time.

"A plate like this might make me change loyalties," he said.

"Shoot boy, this ain't nothing," Miss Darla said. "You should see this table on Thanksgiving."

"So y'all still celebrate the old traditions?" Moses asked.

"They're not old to us," Monica said. "It's what keeps us together."

"And keeps us sane," Darrell added.

"That's what's wrong with folks," Miss Darla said. "They ain't got no foundation since the Collapse. Trying to make up new rules for an old world."

"There are some rules that need to be forgotten," Moses said.

Miss Darla nodded as she cut her chicken breast into slices.

"You sound like your daddy," Miss Darla said. "Burn it all down and start over again!' he used to say."

"Seems we did that," Moses said.

"They did, and look what we ended up with," Darrell said.

They ate in silence, which is what good food usually does to hungry people. The conversation picked up as everyone finished their food.

"When to you plan on heading out?" Miss Darla asked Moses.

"First thing in the morning," he said. "There's someone waiting for me near the I-16/I-95 junction."

"You left someone there?" Monica said.

Moses finished his chicken.

"Yeah. He's good."

"You should have brought him with you."

"He's Watkin's man,' Moses said. "He was sent to keep an eye on me. If he's alive when I get back that's all well and good. If not, oh well."

"You're a cold man," Monica said.

"It's a cold world," Moses said.

"So how can we trust you?" Darrell said.

Moses looked up into Darrell's questioning eyes.

"Because I'm a man of my word," Moses said. "When I make a deal, it's a bond."

"You made a deal with Watkins," Darrell said.

"And I'm making good on it," Moses replied. "I told him I was going to contact you and offer his deal. I did."

Darrell smiled. "You trying to be slick."

"My loyalty is to myself," Moses said. "I do what is best for me. That's how you survive in the Wild."

He glanced at Miss Darla. She nodded in agreement.

"The world is changing," Monica said. "You have to start thinking about others."

"That's why I'm here," Moses said. "I could be halfway to the Panhandle by now."

Darrell and Monica laughed.

"That's the last place you want to go," Darrell said. "It's like the Collapse happened yesterday down there."

"Still a lot of work to be done," Miss Darla said.

"Don't start, mama," Monica said.

"Don't be trying to tell me what to do," Miss Darla snapped back. "I'm not that old."

Monica smiled. "Yes, ma'am."

Moses had enough of the discussion. He wiped his mouth with his napkin before pushing his chair back and standing.

"Thank you for the meal," he said. "I think I've had enough of deep thinking for the day. I'd like to get to sleep early tonight. Long days ahead."

"We understand," Miss Darla said.

"You know the way," Monica said.

It looked like both Monica and Darrell were as tired of his company as he was of theirs. He left the house then sauntered back to the barn and up to his room. As he undressed, he mulled over the conversation. The world was definitely changing. More people were feeling bold enough to establish homestead and towns like the Freedom Fighters. But the threat was still out there. People like Jamal still preyed on the weak, molding them into large factions where people gave up their freedom for safety. As he lay down on his cot a thought came to him. He could say the hell with everybody and disappear into the Wild. Like he said at the supper table, his only loyalty was to himself. He could survive; he'd done it before and it was how he grew up. But he was human. He craved companionship, and struggling towns like where he lay provided that. Still, it was a tough choice to make.

It was a rough night, Moses falling in and out of sleep thinking about his next move. He decided to continue the mission, if only to be a person of his word. He woke early, dressed and gathered his gear. As he descended the barn stairs, he met Monica.

"Good," she said. "You're not a late sleeper."

"Never have been," Moses said. "Late sleepers never wake."

Monica laughed.

"Mama says that, too."

They exited the barn.

"Darrell's taking you back," Monica said. "It was good having you here. Always nice to hear what's happening out in the world."

"Things are definitely changing," Moses said. "I'm still not sure if it's for the best."

"We can't keep running and hiding," Monica said. "At some point we have to start living. That's what we're made for."

"Sometimes, I'm not sure," Moses replied.

A small truck sped up the dirt driveway then stopped before them. Darrell peered through the window.

"Let's go," he said.

Moses climbed into the truck and they set off for the highway.

"I don't care what my mama says, I don't want see your ass in Freedom again," Darrell said.

"You won't," Moses replied. "I've done what I came to do. I hope you won't let your opinion of me affect the offer from Newlanta. Good people run that city. People just like you."

Darrell understood the meaning in Moses's words.

"I'll do what mama says," Darrell said.

It was a tense ride to the main road. Another truck waited at the junction, heavily armed and armored. Moses climbed out of Darrell's truck, inspecting his new ride. It was impressive, which meant he'd only seen a glimpse of what Freedom possessed.

The driver, a short stout woman, dressed in a long-sleeve plaid shirt and jeans, tipped her helmet to Darrell. Darrell gave Moses an AK-47 with four clips. Moses wasn't a fan of the weapon, but it was either that or just his Sigs.

"Take him to 16," Darrell said to the driver. "He's on his own after that."

"Yes sir," she said.

The woman walked up to Moses then extended her hand. Moses took it and they shook.

"I'm Sergeant Williams," the woman said.

"Moses Pritchard."

"Good to meet you."

"You're in better hands than you deserve," Darrell said. "Williams will get you where you're going. She's one of our best drivers."

"Begging your pardon, sir. I'm the best driver." Williams flashed a gap-toothed grin.

Darrell laughed. "I stand corrected."

Williams waved at Moses.

"Let's take a ride," she said.

Moses climbed in. The truck was heavily armored on the inside as well. Although there were gun mounts on the top of the truck, there was no room for a gunner. Moses waited for Williams to climb inside and start the truck before commenting.

"Missing a few people, aren't you?"

"Nope," Williams replied. "This is all me."

She slid a panel aside to reveal a viewscreen which displayed images outside the truck.

"Nice," Moses said.

Williams placed her thumbs on pads opposite each other on her steering wheel. She moved her thumbs about and the guns swiveled.

"I control everything from here," she said. "Ain't nothing I can't see and ain't nothing I can't shoot."

"I'm impressed," Moses replied. "Be interesting to see how it works in a real fight."

"It works just fine," Williams said with a wink. "You can ask the Knights."

Williams revved the engine then steered onto the highway. The ride was rough, but there were bound to be compromises in vehicle performance.

"Now that we're on our own," Williams said. "We can be less formal. My name's Tanisha."

"Pleased to meet you, Tanisha."

"Word is you're from Robbins."

"I'm not from there," Moses said. "Just working."

"Some real bad asses up there," Tanisha said. "Looking forward to squaring off with them."

"Luckily that's not going to happen," Moses replied. "I came to offer a truce and Miss Darla accepted."

"Truce? Fuck! It's been a while since me and Bertha mixed it up. I was looking forward to it."

"We'll you'll have to wait a bit longer," Moses replied.

"What about the Knights?" Tanisha asked. "Y'all offering them a truce, too?"

"No," Moses replied.

Tanisha grinned. "Hot damn! I'd rather fight those racist bastards. Never understood why Miss Darla got in bed with them sons-a-bitches."

"Some of us only fight when we have to," Moses said.

"Well, I ain't some of us," Tanisha said.

Moses didn't reply. There were always people like Tanisha, people that enjoyed battle. They got off on it, a natural high that didn't dissipate until they were laying on their backs bleeding out or trying to hold their guts in. Moses met a few of them during his life. Most of them were dead.

Tanisha steered the armored truck up the highway, weaving off and on the paved road to take the smoothest route.

"You know this road well," Moses commented.

"I patrol it," Tanisha replied. "I know every inch of it. I know the hot spots and the ambush points. Ain't nothing that goes on here that surprises me."

"Tell me about the Knights."

"Crazy fuckers," Tanisha replied. "Flying them damn stars and bars talking about a new white empire. Thinking we're going to be working their fields and calling them 'massa.' Well, they learned better ten years ago at Nashville.

"What happened in Nashville?"

Tanisha grinned. "We got word that the Dixie Boys and the Knights were gathering to attack us. They were meeting in Nashville to coordinate the attack and divide the spoils. Nashville was deep in Dixie Boy territory so they thought it was safe. They didn't consider Miss Bertha."

"You did a blitzkrieg?" Moses said.

"Damn right we did! We built twelve trucks just like Bertha, loaded them up with fuel and ammo then did a run right into them. When we left the whole city was on fire. Half the Knights command and all the Dixie Boys were dead. As a matter of fact the Dixie Boys were done after that. The Knights have been mostly quiet since then."

"Mostly?" Moses asked.

Tanisha looked around as if there was someone else in the truck that wouldn't like what she was about to say.

"I guess I can tell you, since you're leaving," she said. "They've been trying to pick a fight lately, but Darrell's been turning the other cheek. He don't want to start nothing because he knows Miss Darla won't be happy."

"I wonder if it had anything to do with the ambush I witnessed."

"Can't say," Tanisha replied. "That's above my pay grade."

"So, Darrell's in charge of security?"

"Yep, and he's good at it, too. Only thing wrong is that Darrell don't know everything either. We patrollers keep our own secrets."

Moses grinned. "So there have been some firefights?"

"Damn right," Tanisha said. "I was in one last week. Knights have been probing the perimeter looking for weak points. See, we patrollers make sure we stay close enough so we can respond if someone is taking fire. I can have another unit with me in five minutes."

"Five minutes is an eternity in a firefight," Moses said.

"You ain't never lied!" Tanisha replied. "Me and Bertha here make that five minutes of hell for anyone coming after us. Took out a patrol two days ago trying to sneak up on the Gaskins farm. Mowed'em down. Buried the bodies just on the other side of the borderline with them Knights watching. Funny as hell."

It looked as if Jamal's intervention was coming just in time for the Freedom Fighters. The trick would be stopping the attack at the Freedom Fighter border. He had no idea if Jamal planned to honor his deal, and if he did, for how long. He couldn't get Newlanta involved directly. He would have to implement his solution as soon as possible to prevent that from happening.

Tanisha talked the rest of the drive while Moses contemplated his options. This assignment was getting beyond his expertise. He was a gunman, not a strategist, but this situation was going to take some detailed planning and timing to get the outcome he wanted. His original plan was simple: go to Robbins, find Jamal then kill him. But learning about the drones changed his plans. It was bad enough that Jamal had them; in another warlord's hands it would be catastrophic.

"Shit."

Moses looked up. Three burning cars stretched across the highway, the smoke obscuring the view around them. Tanisha picked up her communicator.

"B team? This is Big Bertha. Looks like we have a situation on 95. I'm ten miles north of Freedomtown near the old Hinesville exit."

"Turn around," a heavy voice replied.

"Can't do that," Tanisha replied as she winked at Moses. "I got precious cargo."

"Closest truck is De'Andre. It'll take him at least ten minutes. Your cargo can be delivered tomorrow."

"That makes sense," Moses said.

Tanisha frowned. "Can't do it. I'll wait."

Moses frowned. This was not a good move.

"Let me out," he said.

Tanisha eyes went wide.

"You got a death wish?"

"If you're determined to keep going, you'll need some help. Let me out and give me five minutes."

Tanisha shrugged. She turned the vehicle sideways.

"Good luck," she said.

Moses grinned. "Luck's got nothing to do with it."

He jumped from the truck then ran into the nearby woods, continuing to run until he was a few yards from the road. He crept through the woods toward the burning roadblock, checking his watch as he moved. After two minutes he was behind the wreckage. What he saw changed his mind. A fleet of various vehicles hid behind the smoke, a ragged collection of cars, truck, and motorbikes filled with armed people. This wasn't a shakedown roadblock, this was an attack. Moses ran as fast as he could back to Big Bertha. He snatched open the door then jumped inside.

"Get the fuck out of here!" he shouted.

"What the . . ."

An explosion rocked the truck, knocking it up on two wheels. Moses's head slammed against the roof, stunning him. His eyes cleared to vehicles swarming from behind the roadblock. Rounds bounced off Bertha's armor. He looked to see Tenisha with a crazed expression.

"It's on now, motherfuckers!"

The cabin filled with the sound of automatic gunfire as Tanisha blasted their attackers. Two attacking vehicles swerved then ran into others causing a pile up in front them.

"How about that shit, bitches!" Tanisha shouted.

Moses shoved the woman's head.

"Get us out of here!"

Tanisha snapped out of her battle craze.

"Yeah, right. Got you."

Tanisha pressed the accelerator then cut the wheel hard. The truck lurched forward, spun around then sped down the road. Light from the multiscreen display lit up the cabin as Moses looked out the windows at their pursuers. Tanisha didn't lie, she was an expert. She dodged the road damage while shooting with precision and constraint, holding off the horde. Two motorbikes broke the pack, both carrying two riders. One rider steered, the other carried a rocket launcher.

"Where is everyone getting all this shit?" Moses whispered.

"You got two coming up fast!" he shouted.

Tanisha worked the cannons but couldn't hit them.

"They're too fast!" she said.

"Unlock the doors!" Moses replied.

He heard the click of the doors unlocking. Holding his AK-47 in his right hand, he pushed opened the left side door as the motorbike pulled parallel to Bertha. A quick burst sent the bike tumbling, the driver with two rounds in his face. He slammed the door, spun around then opened the right door. The motorbike was cruising with them, the rider bringing her rocket launcher to bear on them. Moses and the rider pulled the trigger simultaneously. He slammed the door.

"Brace yourself!" he shouted.

The rocket exploded, the blast knocking the truck sideways. It rolled, Tanisha and Moses battered against the hard interior. When it stopped they were upright. Moses lay stunned for a moment then slowly regained control. Tanisha was slumped against the steering wheel, a mean gash across her forehead.

"Nisha! Nisha!" a voice called from the communicator. "We're almost there!"

Moses grabbed the communicator.

"Nisha's out," he said. "We're immobile. Don't come down the road; swing wide on the perimeter. You'll catch them in a crossfire."

"What about y'all?" the voice asked.

"We'll work it out."

Moses didn't have time to treat Tanisha's wounds. The viewports were still functional; he slid Tanisha from the front seat then grabbed the wheel. The top gun canopy was damaged; Moses moved the gun controls and the turret responded. He climbed in the back, reloaded the guns then clambered back into the driver seat. 9mm rounds pinged off the dense armor while 20mm rounds rocked Bertha like a metal swing. Moses reloaded the guns then waited. The ambush vehicles circled the truck then most of the occupants exited their vehicles, sure the occupants were dead or dying.

"Make this quick!" one of them said.

"We're almost there!" the person on the communicator said.

"Wait until I start firing," Moses said.

Moses fingers hovered over the press pad, waiting for the interlopers to get closer. The first sweep needed to count. They were only a few meters from the truck when he pressed the pads and worked the swivel stick. Ambushers fell immediately, those not taking rounds scrambling back to their vehicles. The patrollers appeared moments later and opened fire. Chaos ensued as the ambushers attempted reach their vehicles. Moses kept firing until the raiders were pinned down in the crossfire. He grabbed the communicator.

"Cease fire!" he said.

"Who put you in charge?" the voice answered back.

"Right now, they think they're outnumbered. These are raiders. They'll haul ass if you let them."

"Makes sense."

The firing ceased, replaced by the sound of revving engines and screeching tires. Moses searched the truck and found a first aid kit. He wiped the blood from Tanisha's forehead, cleaned the wound then applied gauze and tape to keep it in place. Tanisha opened her eyes then immediately squinted in pain.

"Ow."

"We took a little tumble," Moses said.

"How's Bertha?"

"A bit beat up," Moses replied. "She'll live. I don't know about you though."

Tanisha sat up straight.

"What? Did I get shot? How bad?"

Moses laughed.

"You're good except for this cut on your head. You probably have a concussion, too."

Tanisha patted herself down then touched Moses makeshift bandage and winced. After her inspection she punched Moses in the chest.

"Hey!"

"Fucking with me," she replied, a grin on her face.

Someone banged on the side of the truck.

"Nisha! Nisha!"

Tanisha reached by Moses and opened the door. An umber skinned man with a graying beard and sunglasses peered inside. He smiled at Tanisha as he cut a sideways look at Moses.

"Gee! Bring your kit. Nisha's got a boo boo."

Tanisha and Moses laughed.

Moses and the man helped Tanisha out the truck. Gee, a lanky man with light brown smooth skin and a bald head sauntered up with a first aid kit. He squatted before Tanisha and replaced Moses makeshift bandage with something much more effective.

"Damn sister," he said. "This is one helluva fight you picked."

"You know me," Tanisha replied. "Go big or go home."

The man who helped Moses carry Tanisha out of the truck walked up to Moses then extended his hand.

"I'm Kerry Westberry," the man said. "You must be the precious cargo."

Moses shook the man's hand. "Moses Pritchard. And just so you know, I told her to turn around."

"Like that was going to work," Kerry replied. "If you cut off Nisha's arms, she'd pick a fight with a snake."

Moses laughed. He liked Kerry.

"I guess we'll be heading back," Moses said.

"Guess so," Kerry replied. "Damn raiders are probably regrouping up the road."

His eyes drifted away from Moses and he scowled. Moses looked over his shoulder and spotted a lone truck on the median. Two men stepped out the truck dressed in gray uniforms and helmets. One of them cupped his hands over his mouth.

"Y'all boys okay?" he shouted.

Kerry stepped by Moses.

"We're fine," he shouted. "We got it under control."

"Let us know if you need any help!"

"Will do," Kerry shouted back.

He turned back to Moses.

"Fuckers," he said.

"Knights?" Moses asked.

"Yep. So much for allies. They probably watched the whole thing. I wouldn't be surprised if they set up the whole thing."

"That's what I'm thinking," Moses said.

Kerry turned to the others.

"Let's get out of here before we're in another fight." He looked at Moses. "Can you drive this thing?"

"I can do it," Tanisha said. She stood up then winced and sat back down.

"I got it," Moses said.

Kerry nodded. "Good. Follow us. And stay diligent."

Moses helped Tanisha into the passenger seat then climbed into the driver's seat. He started the truck then familiarized himself with the controls. By the time the other trucks began leaving he was set.

"Don't you hurt my Bertha," Tanisha warned.

"After what your Bertha just went through, I doubt if I can do worse."

Tanisha grinned. "She's a good woman. I built her well."

Moses nodded. "Yes, you did."

The convoy took their time returning to Freedom Town. Moses glanced to the roadside and saw what Kerry warned him about. Knight vehicles trailed them along the road edge, with more hidden behind the trees. Moses moved the gun pads, pointing his guns in their direction. The other vehicles did the same. Tanisha grinned.

"That's what I'm talking about," she said. "I wish they would bring their redneck asses this way."

The attention had the desired effect. The Knights vehicles veered away, fading into the nearby woods. As they reached the borderland their unwanted followers were gone. Instead of continuing back to the main town, the patrollers went off road. Moses followed them to a small camp a few miles beyond the border. The trucks parked on a hardpacked lot near a large shed. They were swarmed by mechanics and other personnel. A team rushed over to Bertha and Tanisha broke out of her calmness.

"Get the hell away from my truck!" she shouted.

The team raised their hands in surrender then backed away, disappointment clear on their faces. Moses grinned as he shook his head.

Tanisha had opened the passenger door and was climbing out.

"Always trying to touch my shit!" she grumbled. Moses climbed out and joined her.

"You need to get some attention for that wound," he said.

"Not before I check out Bertha," Tanisha replied.

She ran her palms along the armor.

"Poor girl. They really gave it to you. But you handled it, didn't you? Just like your mama you did."

She gave Moses a sidelong look.

"You can touch her," she said then smiled. Moses got the hint. He placed his hand on the armor then smiled.

"Tough and sexy," he said. "That's what she is."

Tanisha's eyes narrowed as her smile grew.

"You have no idea, Mr. Moses."

"Tanisha Grimes, what the hell are you doing?"

An older woman wearing a green fatigue jumpsuit strode toward them, a frown on her light brown face.

"Trying to get me some," Tanisha replied.

The woman's pleasant face scrunched up.

"You're so vulgar! Get away from that truck and that man and let me take a look at you."

"Yes, mama," she said.

Tanisha walked over to mama and gave her a hug. Mama placed her hand on Tanisha's chin then tilted her head back. She lifted the bandage.

"Lord Jesus," she said. "Let's get you inside. You probably have a slight concussion, too."

"I feel fine, mama."

"That's not your place to say. I'm the doctor. I'll tell you how you feel."

Mama looked at Moses like a mother sizing up a new suitor. She extended her hand and they shook.

"Shanika Grimes," she said.

"Moses Pritchard."

"I heard about you. You're the gunman with the peace offer."

Moses nodded.

"Thank you for bringing my baby home. She's my only one."

"You're welcome, ma'am."

Shanika smiled.

"My daughter seems to like you. Whatever you do, don't get her pregnant."

"What?"

"You heard me." Shanika pulled Tanisha toward the medical tent.

"Come on, baby. Let's take care of this."

Moses followed at a distance. He suffered a few bumps and bruises but wanted to be sure none of it was serious. One of the medics gave him a quick exam then sent him on his way with a couple of pain pills. He found the patrollers gathered around their vehicles discussing the firefight. They fell silent when he joined them.

"Don't mind me," Moses said. "I'd go somewhere else but you're the only people I know."

Everyone smiled.

"You're one of us now," Kerry said.

"That's good to hear," Moses replied. "Any chance I can get a motorbike and some fuel?

Kerry's eyes widened. "You going back out there?"

Moses nodded. "It's the best time. Those rogues are licking their wounds."

Kerry shrugged. "It's your funeral. Tanisha will be disappointed."

"I doubt that," Moses said.

"Follow me."

Moses trailed Kerry to the motor pool. After a short conversation with the lead mechanic he led Moses to the lot. There were eight motorbikes of various colors. Moses chose the one with camouflage paint. The mechanic bolted extra fuel tanks on both sides of the bike near the rear tire.

"They run on alcohol," the mechanic said. "Not that you can find and gas worth a shit these days."

"I appreciated it," Moses said.

"No problem. Nobody around here cares too much for bikes. Glad to see one of mine get some use."

Moses inspected the bike to make sure everything was in order. As he looked over the bike Kerry trailed him.

"Hey Kerry, these road ambushes happen often?"

"Not really," Kerry replied. "It's been busy the past few weeks though."

"Which way they're heading?"

"South, mostly," Kerry replied.

Moses hesitated for a moment then continued his inspection. He'd seen this pattern before, and it wasn't a good sign. As much as he wanted to investigate, he had to stay focused. Too many lives depended on him returning to Newlanta. As foreboding as his thoughts were, they would have to wait for later.

He shook Kerry's hand before climbing on the bike and starting it. The engine idled with a strong and steady hum.

"Be careful, killer," Kerry said.

Moses grinned. "I never am."

Moses weaved through the camp and back to the highway. As he surmised, the road was empty except for burning vehicles and the dead. He made good time back to the junction of 16 and 95, hoping Jimmy was still waiting for him but knowing that would most likely not be the case. He rode the motorbike into the woods where he last left Jimmy then searched for signs of a campsite. He was about to give up the search when he spotted a vehicle in the distance. Moses rode up to the site. It was Jimmy's truck. Jimmy's body lay beside it. Moses stopped the bike then dismounted. He knelt by the body.

"Shit. I'm so sorry, bruh."

He didn't have a shovel so he couldn't bury him. Instead he gathered leaves, straw and branches and covered the body. He checked the vehicle; it was still in running condition. He loaded the motorbike inside then detached one of the fuel tanks. After driving the truck a safe distance away, he poured alcohol over the makeshift pyre then lit it. He waited until the fire was full before climbing back into the car and heading northwest on 16.

- 6 -

Moses navigated the truck down the slick streets of
Robbins through the summer shower, the worn
window wipers doing a terrible job clearing the
front windshield. It had taken him two days to drive
from the junction back, dodging roaming groups
and blockades. The dangerous journey back confirmed his suspicions. Factions, small groups and
others were on the move south, which meant only
one thing; someone was pushing them.

The truck barely drew any attention until he
reached Jamal's compound. The guards draped in
rain ponchos at the gates raised their hands and
Moses stopped. He rolled down the window and
showed his papers. The guards studied them then
handed them back quickly to avoid them getting
wet.

"You're late," the guard said.

"Tell me about it," Moses replied.

He drove directly to Jamal's office barracks.
He parked the vehicle then hurried to the door. His
papers were inspected again and he was led to
Jamal's office by a burly assistant. Jamal stood as
the door was opened, a smile on his face.

"So, you're not dead after all," he said.

They shook hands. Jamal cut his eyes at the assistant.

"That will be all," he said.

The man saluted then closed the door. Jamal sat behind his desk and Moses sat before him.

"You came back a little light," Jamal said. "What happened?"

"Your spy tried to kill me," Moses answered. "Apparently she was from Statesboro."

Jamal grinned. "Who better to keep an eye on you. Although I must admit I didn't know she hated you that much. Did you kill her?"

"No," Moses answered, irritated by Jamal's callous attitude. "I gave her a chance to stay on but she walked away.

"She's probably dead," Jamal said. "Things are jumpy right now. What about Jimmy?"

"Dead," Moses said. "I left him behind to watch the vehicle after we contacted the Freedom Fighters. I didn't know I'd be gone that long. When I returned, I found him dead."

"Too bad," Jamal said. "I liked Jimmy."

Jamal sat up resting his forearms on his desk.

"So, do we have an alliance?"

"Yes, we do," Moses replied. "I met the leader of the Freedom Fighters and she agreed to stay neutral during your attack on the Knights. As a matter of fact, they might lend a hand."

"Excellent, although we don't need their interference. Any activity might be seen as hostile and they might get caught in the crossfire."

Moses looked puzzled.

"Your troops can't tell the difference between friend or foe?"

"It won't be that kind of assault," Jamal replied. "We're using the drones."

Moses leaned back in his seat. He'd seen the facilities, but he didn't know Jamal was that close to utilizing the tech.

"That's a big risk," he said.

"I'm not interested in South Georgia," Jamal said. "I needed a field test. If it wasn't the Knights it would be someone else. Check this out."

Jamal got up from his desk and went into his closet, returning with a map. He rolled the document out on his desk, holding the edges with his hands. Moses stood up and gazed at the map. It was a detailed image of Knight territory.

"How the hell did you get that?" he asked. "I can understand the topological info. There are tons of old shit like that lying around. But the barrack locations and weapon caches? How?"

Jamal smiled.

"Cool as shit, isn't it? We've been studying the drones for two years now. The key to their operations is satellite imagery, but only a few people have the tech to access that and we're not one of them. So, we had to figure out a way to map out an area and provide the eyes for our attack units. We discovered we could program the smaller drones as observation points. We can fly them at an altitude that gives us the data we need to guide our ground and air units. We made the map from their data."

Moses scrutinized the map. He noticed not only had the Knights territory been mapped out, but so had the Freedom Fighters.

"The drones can also detect mass movement and hostile activity with heat sensors and motion tech. We don't have it fine-tuned for individual tracking, but we're getting there."

All this was bad news for Newlanta. With this tech Jamal could map out the city and launch surgical strikes with the drones, taking out Newlanta's defenses before moving in with his main force. The city would fall in days, if not hours.

"This is all cool, if it works," he said.

Jamal grinned. "We're about to find out. Good thing you got out of there. We're moving out tonight. The drones are in position giving us real-time feedback and the remote strike team is on its way."

"I'd love to see this go down at the drone center," Moses said.

"You won't," Jamal replied. "I need you to gather your soldiers and move out with the drones. You're our sweep team."

"I just got back!" Moses said.

"Like I said, good timing. Besides, you made friends down there. They'll be happy to see you again."

Another test, Moses thought.

"How many hours do I have?"

"Ten," Jamal replied.

"Well I better move my ass then."

"Go get'em, killer."

Moses shook Jamal's hand instead of saluting him. He marched through the office back to his vehicle then drove to his section. The office bustled with the usual busy work as he entered. It took the workers a moment to recognize him. They stood and saluted. Moses waved them down.

"Listen up. We're moving out in ten hours. Contact our teams and have them assemble in the main courtyard in eight hours, full battle gear."

"Yes, sir," the team answered in unison. They exchanged curious glances. Apparently, Jamal had done a good job keeping his plans secret.

"I'll be in my unit," Moses said.

He left the office and drove to his unit. Instead of going inside he walked to the nearby woods. Making sure he wasn't followed, he pulled out his control unit then summoned Frack. Fifteen minutes later Frack jogged up to him then sat by his feet. Moses linked the comm.

"Moses?" Esmerelda said. Her voice was tentative.

"You were expecting someone else?"

"It's been a while," she said. "We weren't sure you were still with us."

"Sorry to disappoint you," he replied.

Esmerelda laughed. "We've been getting weird signals from you, too.

"I can't explain that. I don't know where Frack's been. I got an update for you."

"Shoot."

"Jamal plans to use the drones to attack the Knights in South Georgia. It's a test run for Newlanta."

"Shit."

"He's figured out how to use smaller drones for observation and mapping. He can pinpoint weapons and gross movements."

"How is he controlling the drones?"

"He's got a control center set up in the same building with virtual pilots. They operate the attack drones based on the feedback from the observation drones."

"Have you seen them in action?"

"I will. My unit will be the cleanup for them. Anything they miss we'll handle."

"Moses?" It was Voorhees.

"Hi Voorhees," Moses said. "Decided to join the conversation?"

"We need visuals on this, real time visuals."

"I can't do that," Moses said. "I'll be in the field."

"We can use Frack," Esmerelda said.

"Who?" Voorhees asked.

"Moses's mobile support unit," she replied. "We call it Frack. I can send Moses instructions for the unit to shadow the drones and record their actions. It will let us know what we're dealing with."

"Sounds like a plan," Voorhees replied.

"That'll be tricky," Moses said. "I've been keeping Frack out of camp, just in case I need extraction."

"You'll have to take that chance," Voorhees said. "We need to know what these drones are capable of."

"Frack will need visual contact with the drones in order to shadow them," Esmerelda said.

"Y'all are just trying to get me killed," Moses said.

"It's the only way," Esmerelda said.

"How long before I have the info?"

"Ten minutes."

"Good. I'll reprogram tonight. The rest I'll figure out tomorrow."

"Good luck," Voorhees said.

"Luck has nothing to do with it," Moses replied.

Moses shut down the comm link. Ten minutes later it flashed, the new programs from Esmerelda loaded. He opened Frack's link console then inserted the comm. The sequence took two minutes. Frack rebooted then stood. Luckily Moses brought his goggles with him. He linked the visuals with Frack then switched it to manual control. Seeing through the unit's visuals, he guided Frack through the camp to the drone facility.

"Sir?"

Moses jumped at the sound of the strange voice. He slipped the control comm into his pocket.

"Can't a man take a piss in peace?" he said.

"Sir, there's a bathroom in your unit."

"Old habits are hard to break."

The guard's eyes went to Moses's goggles.

"What are those?"

"Night goggles," Moses replied. "I use them to study the stars. Too much light pollution in these camps."

The guard wasn't convinced.

"Sir, I'll need you to come with me."

"Shit," Moses said.

He pivoted out of the line of fire on his right foot as he grabbed the barrel of the guard's AK-47. Moses punched the man in the throat then snatched the gun from his loosened grip. The guard fell to the ground choking. He convulsed for a few more moments before falling still.

"Damn it," Moses said. He looked at the man's body, trying to figure out what to do. If he hid it someone would find it; if Jamal's forensics was as good as everything else, it wouldn't take them long to find out he did it.

"Might as well get this over with," he said.

Moses went to his unit and dropped off his equipment before going to the base.

"Is Jamal in?" he asked.

"Yes, sir."

"I'd need to speak to him."

The receptionist went to his office and knocked. Moments later Jamal came strolling up to him.

"You're out late. What's going on?"

Moses handed Jamal the guard's AK-47.

"You're missing a guard," he said.

"What the hell happened?" Jamal asked.

"I was out taking a stroll and he snuck up on me. Instincts took over."

"He was a goddamn guard!" Jamal replied. "That's what he was supposed to do!"

Moses shrugged. Jamal sighed.

"Where is he?"

"By my barracks."

"Take some people with you to retrieve the body. And stop acting like you're in the Wild."

"I'll try," Moses said.

Moses picked a few soldiers to follow him to the guard's body. A few of them recognized the man and gave Moses a hard look before picking him up and carrying him away. He wasn't making friends in the camp; as soon as he got what he needed he would have to go.

He settled in for the night but he didn't sleep well. There were too many things going through his head; the upcoming assault, killing the guard, Freedom Town, and old memories. He was tempted to go out and actually walk but didn't want to risk the chance of running into another guard. He was sure what he did had probably spread through the camp and the next guard might just shoot first and ask questions later. So, he tossed and turned the entire night, grateful when the sun finally broke the horizon.

The strike team gathered as he exited the office. A tall, pale woman with red hair and freckled face approached him, a stern look on her face.

"Commander Pritchard, I'm Captain Lucy Stark. I was asked by Commander Watkins to lead the strike unit in your stead."

Moses smirked. "That's a good idea, captain. Seems I didn't make too many friends last night."

"No sir, you didn't."

"I tell you what, captain. How about you keep the job permanently."

Stark's eyebrows rose. "Sir?"

"Yeah, how about you command the team from here on out? Let's be real. Watkins is a friend and he thinks he's doing me a favor. Truth is I'm not the leader type. So you keep running the team and I'll take the credit as long as I'm here. I'll tell the commander what a wonderful job you're doing and at some point, he'll make it official. How does that sound to you?"

"Uh . . . wow . . . it sounds good, sir," Stark replied.

"Good. Now let's get going."

The team loaded their personnel carriers. Moses climbed into an armored car with Stark. The strike team traveled a few miles outside the compound before Moses called for a halt.

"What are we waiting for?" Stark asked.

"The drones," Moses replied.

Stark looked puzzled. "The what?"

The sound of approaching vehicles answered Stark's question. The drone tanks rumbled by the strike team then formed a single file as they rolled down the road. Moments later hover drones flew overhead, catching up with the tanks. Stark looked wide-eyed at the drones then looked at Moses.

"Sir, what the hell did I just see?"

Moses grinned. "The future. Let's move out."

The strike team followed the drones. They covered half the distance to Knights territory in one day, traveling much faster than Moses did during his trip. The night camp buzzed with talk about the drones. Jamal had done well keeping that secret. The troops peppered him with questions but he played dumb. The drones had continued to the objective. Apparently, Jamal was working the controllers in shifts in order to press the attack. As the backup units woke that morning to continue their journey, Moses was awakened by a different alarm.

"Where are you?" Jamal said into his earpiece.

"We're breaking camp now," he replied. "We should reach Knights territory by this afternoon."

"Take your time," he said. "Your support mission had become a cleanup operation."

Moses eyes went wide.

"You attacked?"

"Yep," Jamal said. "We hit them last night. The thermal sighting worked flawlessly. They didn't know what hit them. Your mission now is to take out any surviving resistance and root out the leaders. I want anyone with any rank brought back to base."

"What about the Freedom Fighters," Moses asked. "Any collateral damage? If there is, we might have a fight on our hands."

"I don't give a rat's ass about the Freedom Fighters," Jamal replied. "With what we did last night they're no more a threat than a cockroach. Let's hope for their sake they don't start any shit. If your unit can't take them, we certainly can. After last night's show, I'm sure they're having second thoughts."

Jamal signed off. Moses ran to his vehicle, his driver close behind.

"Let's move out!" he shouted. "Now!"

The convoy loaded up the hit the road. Moses didn't give a damn about the Knights; whatever happened to them was well deserved. He was nervous about the Fighters. He made a deal with them and if they had been attacked that would ruin any chances of an alliance with Newlanta . . . if they survived. He wanted to be in position when the drones attacked so he could see them in action, but Jamal apparently wanted to keep that under wraps. The best he could do now was access their effectiveness based on evidence.

They spotted columns of smoke a few miles before they reached Knights' territory. The vehicles slowed to a stop a few miles before the unofficial border, the soldiers emptying out and forming around Moses and Stark. When they were all present Moses nodded at Stark. She cleared her throat before speaking.

"We'll work our way to the smoke areas first," she said. "It looks like the drones did good work, but stay on your guard."

"If you encounter Knight fighters try not to engage," Moses interrupted. "We'll need them for interrogation. But if they fight, do what you have to do."

Stark cut a curious eye at Moses before nodding her head in agreement.

"You know your teams," she said. "I want a parallel advance along the entire perimeter. Keep close enough to minimize response time of you get in a jam. Let's go."

The units formed up then spread out. Moses, Stark and their driver stayed behind, watching the others meld into the surrounding pines and oaks. Stark turned to Moses.

"Sir, I don't remember any instructions about interrogations," she said.

"You're not privy to everything," Moses said. "We're not only here to plant the flag; we're here to assess the effectiveness of the drones. Survivors will give us details on the attack from their point of view."

"Makes sense," Stark said. "Will Commander Watkins be joining us?"

Moses smirked. "I'm sure he will. I've never seen the commander miss an opportunity to observe his handiwork."

Ten minutes passed before they received their first communication. Stark switched her comm to broadcast so everyone could here.

"What's up, Eagle team?" she asked.

"We're reached the first strike point," the team leader said.

"What are we looking at?"

"It's totally wiped out," the leader said. "Everything is gone. No survivors."

"You mean fighters?" Moses asked.

"No sir. I mean none," the leader replied. His voice shook. "I mean everything."

Stark looked at Moses as if expected an explanation. Moses didn't give one.

"Continue to sweep the area," Moses said. "Contact us if you find any survivors."

"I doubt that's going to happen, sir," the team leader replied.

The other teams reported in with similar stories. The drones had scoured their targets, killing everything that moved; fighters, men, women, children, pets and livestock. Moses, Stark and the driver climbed into their Humvee, driving between the teams and documenting the devastation. The more Moses saw, the more he realized Newlanta was in serious trouble. There was nothing he'd seen in the city that would withstand this type of attack. Most warlords were precise in their attacks; people were just as valuable as the resources they controlled. Apparently, Jamal had other ideas. Either he had decided to go for a scorched earth policy and re-populated the areas with his own people or the drones were not as precise as he hoped.

They were inspecting a small town flattened by the attack when the call from Fox Team came in.

"This is Fox Team! We are under attack! Repeat, we are under attack!"

The team's coordinates appeared seconds later; Stark shared them with the other teams and they converged on Fox Team's position. The surviving Knights were holed up in a sprawling farm. They'd formed a perimeter with hay bales and farm equipment, then occupied the home, barns and other buildings. Fox Team had pulled back to the tree line. Moses jumped out of the Humvee as soon as they arrived, Stark running behind him. The Fox team leader met him as he approached, a tall, slender man with light brown skin and a crooked mouth.

"What's the situation?" he asked.

"We were advancing across the fields when we took fire," the man said.

"Causalities?" Moses asked.

"Three, sir," the man replied.

"I told you to be diligent," Stark said.

"Too late for that," Moses replied. "No reason to bitch about it. Do we have a way to communicate with them?"

"Yes, sir," Stark said. She touched her comm. "Crow Team, we need your amp."

"Yes, ma'am."

As they waited for Crow Team to deliver the amp, Moses made notes. The Knights' farm was near the border of Knights and Freedom Fighters territory, which meant Jamal kept his word. It also meant that the massacre of the Knights was deliberate. Jamal was setting an example that he hoped would discourage anyone else from resisting him, including Newlanta.

Crow Team arrived with their amp. Moses took the mike.

"Attention Knights! This commander Moses Pritchard. There is no need for this to continue. All we ask is that you come forward and lay down your weapons. You will not be harmed."

Moses waited ten minutes before making the same announcement. Another ten minutes passed before a chorus of rebel yells and curses rose from the buildings.

"Shit," Moses said. "Don't do it."

The sound of revving engines and gunfire accompanied the shouting.

"Okay everybody, get ready . . ."

"Moses?"

It was Jamal.

"What's going on?"

Moses was hesitant to answer. Stark looked at him suspiciously.

"We have a group of Knights holed up in a farm house near the Freedom Fighter border."

"Check. Stand clear," Jamal replied. "Give me the coordinates."

Moses hesitated.

"30 degrees north, 7 degrees northwest," Stark answered.

Seconds later rockets whooshed over their position then slammed into the buildings. The drones swooped in like metal hawks, peppering the buildings in with Gatling fire. The rumble of armored vehicles rose from behind their positions and they were suddenly swarmed by drone tanks that sped across the open fields firing cannons and machine guns. The farm was fully ablaze in seconds, the drones moving in and hunting down the survivors. The tanks and flying drones withdrew as soon as they arrived. Moses and the others stood stunned.

"Oh my God," Stark said.

The drones finished their grim work in minutes.

"Moses?"

Moses reached slowly for his comm.

"Yeah."

"Not bad, huh?"

Moses didn't answer.

"Newlanta is next. But you won't be able to see that."

Moses jerked up his head. Stark and the others had their guns trained on him. He raised his hands; Moses was good, but he wasn't that good. He shook his head as he grinned. He should have killed Jamal and jetted back to Newlanta when he had the chance. That was the plan. But he got ambitious. He tapped his comm.

"So much for that," he said.

"No, you don't get off that easy," Jamal said. "My soldiers are going to bring you back, and we're going to have a long, painful conversation. See, I'm pretty sure that Newlanta has nothing in its back pocket that can stop me, but I want to be absolutely sure. And you're going to get me there."

"We'll see," Moses replied.

"I told you I was going to kill you," a familiar voice said. The soldiers stepped aside and the smirking woman sauntered up to him.

Moses closed his eyes and shook his head.

"Keys."

"Surprise, motherfucker," Keys said.

"So, you're working with the man who wiped out your city," Moses replied. "What a way to honor your people."

"Kiss my ass!" Keys replied. "He gave the order. You carried it out. Your way."

Moses couldn't argue.

"I thought I taught you better killer," Jamal said. "Guess not. Should have took her out when you had the chance. We'll see you soon."

Stark motioned with her gun. Moses handed over his weapons then turned with his hands behind his back. Another soldier tied them. A truck arrived moments later.

"Get in," Stark ordered.

Moses climbed in the back. Once he settled, he smiled.

"No hard feelings?" he said.

Stark knocked him out with the butt of her rifle.

- 7 -

Moses awoke with pain in his head and blood in his mouth. He lay on his side against metal shrouded in darkness. His last memory was Stark hitting him with the rifle, which accounted for the headache and the bleeding mouth. It took him a minute to sit up because of his tied hands but he managed to do it. The convoy had apparently stopped for the night. Moses was famished but he figured no one cared if he ate or not. He was a traitor; the weaker he arrived back at the base the better. It would take Jamal less time to beat the info he wanted out of him. The only thing was that was not going to happen.

The moment he was outed he hit the signal in his pocket, activating Frack's search mode. The unit would find him; he just hoped it did so before he reached base. It would do its best on stealth mode but its chances on being discovered were much less out in the Wild. He had no idea whether it had followed them to the Knights' stronghold, but he hoped so. Moses wasn't much for pain and he didn't know anything about Newlanta's defenses. He was going to be tortured for nothing. At least that's how he saw it.

He slid to the back of the truck then peered through the grated rear gate. Most of the soldiers appeared to be sleeping. A guard snoozed near the truck; apparently they didn't think he would try to escape. That was stupid.

A red light glowed in his pocket, indicating that Frack was near. Moses would have to get out of the truck, but with his hands and feet tied that would be difficult. He'd need help. He lay on his back then kicked the gate hard.

"Hey! Hey!"

He heard the guard snort.

"What the fuck?"

The man stomped over to the truck.

"What?!"

Moses smiled. "I need to take a piss."

"Piss on yourself," the guard retorted.

"Come on, man," Moses said. "When I get to base, they're going to torture me. At least let me have some dignity before then."

The guard let down the gate then untied Moses' feet. Moses worked his way out of the truck bed. The guard stepped back, his gun trained on Moses.

"Okay. Piss."

Moses shrugged. "No privacy?"

The guard looked around then motioned his gun toward a nearby tree.

"Over there."

Moses sauntered over to the tree. When he arrived, he looked over his shoulder.

"You gonna do the honors?"

The man sucked his teeth. He was about to open his mouth when Frack slammed into him, knocking him to the ground. The man lay unconscious. The unit scanned Moses then trotted into the darkness, Moses running behind it. They ran until they were three miles from the camp. Once they were far enough away Moses knelt, placing his tied hands before the unit. The unit raised one of its front limbs then severed the cord. Moses flexed his hands then pressed the latch which opened the storage compartment. Inside was a Sig and HK Mp5 with six clips. That was all he needed. Moses had no intentions of running, at least not yet. He had to make sure he wasn't hunted, and he needed time to do what he needed to do. He opened Frack's control unit, reprogramming the unit for attack mode then sent it toward the sleeping soldiers with two clips loaded into its guns. He waited until Frack was on its way before trotting in the opposite direction. After moving a short distance, he sat behind a wide tree then waited.

The night erupted in gunfire and yells. Moses put on his infrared glasses then moved in. Frack was in the center of the camp laying down cover fire and drawing the attention of the soldiers. The unit was heavily armored but could only take so much heavy fire, so he didn't have much time. Moses slung the HP behind his back and advanced with the Sig. This was going to be close action.

The first soldier he took down was the recovering guard. He worked through the camp, following the heat signals to his targets. He'd killed half of the soldiers before they realized the unit wasn't their only attacker. His work became more difficult then. Two soldiers turned toward him and began firing. Moses holstered the Sig and swung the HP around to his hands. Two short bursts and the soldiers were dead. Another soldier ran toward him firing wildly, attempting to escape rather than attack. A round from Frack caught him in the back and sent him sprawling. Moses claimed his rifle and his ammo and continued his grim work. Ten long minutes later the camp lay silent. Moses kept hidden and he surveyed his work, making sure every last soldier had been killed. Frack stood motionless, its barrels still glowing. When Moses finally stood it shifted in his direction.

"Stand down," he said.

The unit folded its legs and assumed a prone position. Moses did a walk through until he found Stark's body. Keys lay nearby, a stunned look frozen on her lifeless face. He searched Stark until he found the keys to the Humvee. Gathering a few more guns and ammo cartridges, he loaded then sent Frack into tracking mode. Night travel was dangerous, but between him and Jamal the territory he wished to travel had been cleared. He had a plan, but in order to pull it off he needed help, and he knew just where to find it.

* * *

Moses waited until the sun had fully risen before entering Freedom Fighter territory. He made no attempt at stealth because he wanted to be seen. Five minutes after crossing the invisible border two patrol vehicles broke from the woods, rolling down the embankment then pulling alongside him. Moses slowed the Humvee then stopped.

"Okay," he whispered to himself. "Let's see if they still like me."

He stepped out of the Humvee with his hands raised. Two patrollers exited, their faces covered and guns drawn. One touched a comm on the side of his head.

"It's the gunman," he said.

The men stopped as they listened to instructions. After a few moments they lowered their weapons.

"Follow us," the man said.

So far, so good, Moses thought as he climbed back into his vehicle. At least they weren't going to kill him on the road. If he was lucky, he'd get a proper burial.

The patrollers headed down the highway to the familiar exit. The road was void of the busy traffic he'd seen the first time he visited, but it was probably for good reason. The region was most likely on alert after the Knights attack, not that it would do any good. When they reached Miss Darla's farm Moses's suspicions were confirmed. The compound teemed with soldiers and vehicles. To Moses's surprise he saw a few soldiers with ground-to-air rocket launchers and an ancient anti-aircraft gun set up close to the home. As they pulled into the roundabout before the home Darrell emerged, followed by two patrollers. He was not smiling.

Moses climbed out of the Humvee, hand extended. Darrell ignored it.

"Inside, gunman," he said.

Moses followed Darrell through the house to the kitchen. Miss Darla sat at the table, comfortable in a simple house dress and head wrap, her hands clasped together. She looked up at Moses and smiled. Monica sat beside her dressed in fatigues. Her expression was much less inviting.

"Sit down, Moses," Miss Darla said. "Would you like some coffee?"

Moses sat down. "Yes, I would."

"Monica, fix Moses a cup of coffee."

Monica eyes went wide. "Mama, this ain't no damn social visit."

Miss Darla cut her eyes at Monica.

"Don't cuss around me, and do as I told you!"

Monica shoved her seat back then went to the coffeemaker and poured Moses a cup of coffee. She dropped the cup in front of him.

"I hope you take it black," she said.

"I do," Moses replied.

"Everyone out," Miss Darla said. "Me and Moses have some things to discuss."

"Mama . . ." Darrell began.

"I said everyone," Miss Darla repeated. "You and Monica, too."

The others left the kitchen. The smile on Miss Darla's face dissipated.

"That was some show your boss put on," she said.

"Yes, it was," Moses replied.

"How is Newlanta going to prevent the same thing from happening to us?"

"They can't," Moses replied. "I can. But I need your help."

"How are you going to stop all that?" Miss Darla asked.

"By cutting off the head of the snake," Moses replied.

"Explain."

Moses leaned onto the table. "I haven't seen anything in all my years that will stop those drones. If it exists, it's probably in the same bunker where Watkins found them."

"So you want to try to get inside and find out?" Miss Darla asked.

Moses shook his head. "Can't. I've been found out. In about two more days they'll be scouring the land looking for me."

"Which means they'll come here," Miss Darla said.

"I don't think so," Moses replied. "Jamal thinks he knows me. I know where he thinks I'm headed. What I'm planning is going to take perfect timing, and it's going to put some folks at risk. But it's the only way."

"I'd like to be the judge of that," Miss Darla said. "Tell me about it. We've got all day."

Moses sipped his coffee then smiled. "I hoped you would say that."

"What's your plan?"

"The problem is the drones," Moses said. "We don't have the strength to destroy them. They're located in the center of Jamal's base and it's too well protected. But we can take out the controllers. We can send in a team for that purpose only. It will take Jamal time to retrain more."

"That still doesn't eliminate the threat," Miss Darla said. "He'll find more operators and train them."

"Not if he's dead," Moses said.

Miss Darla smirked then took a sip of her coffee.

"So you'll finally do what you were sent to do."

Moses laughed. "Sometimes things get complicated."

"They do indeed. I'd like to change your plan a bit."

"I'm listening," Moses said.

"If we wait until Jamal is distracted, we can launch a full attack on the base. It will be unexpected, so not only do we take out the controllers, we'll have enough troops to destroy the drones as well."

"But that means waiting until he attacks Newlanta," Moses said.

Miss Darla nodded. Moses sat up straight.

"That's what I was sent to prevent."

"What you're planning is temporary," Miss Darla said. "Say you kill the controllers and Jamal. Who's to say someone else won't step in to take his place? Who's to say that someone won't restart the program? As long as those drones exist, they're a threat. Now, Jamal doesn't expect us to make a move so I suspect he'll commit most of his forces toward the Newlanta assault. That would make it the best time to strike."

Moses rubbed his chin. It was a good plan, but it meant letting Jamal attack the city. People would die, lots of them, maybe some he knew. And if their plan didn't work . . .

"I don't think I can do that," he said.

Miss Darla's face became stern.

"It doesn't matter if you do or not. We're going to."

"You can't . . ."

Miss Darla slammed her palm on the table and Moses jumped. The others entered the room, guns drawn.

"Don't ever try to tell me what I can't do!" she said. "We decided we were going to move the moment the Knights went down. There's no way on God's green earth are we going to sit still and let someone come to send us to Glory. We're Freedom Fighters. We Fight. Now either you're going to help us you're going to get the hell out of our way, gunman."

"What are you going to do if I don't?" Moses asked, his voice calmer than he actually felt.

Miss Darla leaned back into her seat. She sipped her coffee.

"Nothing. The most you'll do is go to New-lanta and tell them what we're planning. From what you've told me about this Voorhees, he won't attack. He believes his walls will protect him. Or you'll go back to Jamal's base and do what you were sent to do, but now it's difficult because they'll be on the lookout for you. Either way we get the distraction we need."

Moses could see there was no way he was going to change Miss Darla's mind.

"At least let me get word to Voorhees," Moses said. "They should at least have time to prepare."

"That seems fair," Monica said.

"Can you arrange communication between me and Voorhees?" Miss Darla asked.

"Yep," Moses replied.

"Do it."

Moses finished his coffee then stood.

"We'll have to go outside," he said.

Miss Darla stood. "Lead the way."

Moses left the kitchen, the others following close behind, their guns still pointed at him. Moses felt his handguns brushing against his back and against his calves. He could probably shoot his way out of this situation, but the Freedom Fighters weren't the enemy. Besides, Miss Darla's plan was good, and if it was successful it would take Jamal and his army out and form an alliance that would stretch almost the entire length of I-75. If they could link up with Shakira and Fox Valley it would be a solid union and a real chance for some kind of peace in Georgia. It was worth a shot.

Moses led them to the clearing in the center of the roundabout. He took the comm from his pocket then pressed the homing button. For a moment there was nothing; Moses saw the skepticism on their faces. Someone shouted on the edge of the circle and the others parted. Frack trotted up to him then sat by his feet. He could tell by the look on Miss Darla's face that she was impressed.

"You've been holding out on us," she said. "Any more secrets?"

"No ma'am," Moses replied. "Frack's been my shadow since I left Newlanta. I keep it at a distance just in case I need help getting away."

He pressed the comm button and Frack's eyes projected a holograph field above its head. Moments later Esmerelda appeared.

"Hi Moses, what's...woah! Who do we have here?"

"Hi Essie, meet my new friends," Moses said. "I need to speak to Voorhees."

"Give me a minute," Esmerelda replied.

Exactly one minute later Voorhees's image stood beside Esmerelda.

"Hello, Moses," he said, his voice formal. "To whom do I have the privilege of speaking to?"

Miss Darla stepped forward.

"Darla Simpson, leader of the Freedom Fighters," she said.

"A pleasure to meet you, Commander Simpson."

"Miss Darla will do. I must tell you it warms my heart to see one of us in charge of such a great city like Newlanta."

"All are equal within our walls, Miss Darla," he replied.

"You have that luxury," she said. "Unfortunately, we don't. Old habits die hard in South Georgia."

"The Freedom Fighters have agreed to an alliance with Newlanta," Moses said. "That's the good news. The bad news is that Jamal is about to head your way with an army of drones."

Voorhees took on a sour look. "You told me you could handle it, Moses."

"I thought I could. But things were much bigger than I anticipated. Miss Darla wanted to discuss with you her plan. I think it's a good one, but it's going to take some sacrifice."

Miss Darla explained her idea. Voorhees expression went from sour to dark.

"Impossible," he said. "There's no way I'll allow Watkin's army to come near Newlanta. We'll mobilize immediately and march out to meet him."

"You don't want to do that," Moses replied. "The last place you want to be is out in the open when those drones arrive. They'll pick you apart."

"We have anti-aircraft weapons," Voorhees replied.

"Unless you've been hiding something up your sleeve, you don't have anything that can stop these things. They're fast as hell and highly maneuverable. You have time to prepare."

"We'll send a team to monitor Watkin's base," Miss Darla added. "We'll keep you updated on their progress. As soon as the main force is committed, we'll move in."

"I don't like this plan," Voorhees said.

"Feel free to come up with a better one," Miss Darla replied. "The fact is that Watkins is coming for Newlanta. We can help."

Voorhees was silent for a long moment before responding.

"We'll go with your plan for now," he said. "Keep us informed. Moses, we need you back in Newlanta."

"Can't do that," Moses said. "I'm the only one that knows the layout of Jamal's base. I'm going in with the Freedom Fighters. Besides, I'm just one man. I can't stop a tidal wave, but I can cut a link."

"So be it," Voorhees said. "We'll be in contact."

Voorhees's image faded away.

"I need all our commanders at the farm house immediately," Miss Darla said.

The others saluted then trotted away. She cut her eyes at Moses.

"You stay with me."

Moses saluted. "Yes, ma'am."

Moses followed Miss Darla inside the house. Instead of going to her kitchen, they went to the parlor. Just like the kitchen, the parlor was set up like a cozy room for a family gathering. Two old sofas rested against the wall on either side of the room, with a large marble top table between them. Separate chairs were on both sides of the sofa for more seating. As they sat on the sofa folding chairs were brought in. Two soldiers carried in a salvaged holo platform then sat in on top of the table. Moses grinned.

"I have seen one of those in a while."

"We're not like Newlanta," Miss Darla said. "Not much tech laying around farms and small towns. Not much to salvage, and we don't have anyone with the expertise to build it."

"Ninety percent of Newlanta's tech is salvaged," Moses said. "What they can't dig out they buy from salvagers. Essie's got a great tech team, too."

"I see," Miss Darla said as she looked at Frack.

"Yeah, Frack is special."

"If there's a Frack, there must be a Frick." Miss Darla grinned.

"I'm not holding out," Moses said. "Frick got damaged in a firefight up the road in Macon. Had to use it as a diversion. If this goes well, I'll send a salvage team for it."

"When this goes well," Miss Darla corrected him.

"I love your optimism."

Miss Darla nodded her head. "That's all we got. That and grit. If we didn't think we could thrive, why do it? We might as well go Wild. Newlanta gives us hope."

"Newlanta's not perfect," Moses said.

"Nothing any human has ever made was, nor will be," Miss Darla said. "It's our nature. All we can do is the best we can."

"You sound like my mama."

"Your mama was a good, wise woman. If she had lived, I would have been following her."

"If she had lived . . ." Moses fell into a funk thinking about his parents. They fought so hard for him to have something better, and in a way he did. He had a choice. He just chose wrong.

The others filed into the room and took their seats. Monica and Darrell sat on either side of Miss Darla, their eyes trained on Moses. It was obvious they didn't trust Moses, but Moses didn't care. As long as Miss Darla was on his side, he was good. The others sat, their eyes on Miss Darla.

"I want you best people on this mission," Miss Darla said. "You know who they are."

"The patrollers are the best we got," Darrell said. "This should be their mission. They've worked with Moses and they actually like him."

Miss Darla nodded then looked toward Moses.

"Frack," Moses said.

Frack ambled to Moses. Moses linked Frack to the holo projector. In moments the image of Jamal's base filled the center of the room. The others mumbled.

"The base is widespread and divided into different camps," he began. "There's no barrier preventing anyone from entering, but the guards are familiar of anyone moving in and out of the city, especially soldiers. But we won't be just visiting."

He reached out with his hands and moved the hologram about.

"The drone base is near the center of the camp in the old Robbins Air Force Base. This section does have a gate and is heavily guarded. This is where the fun begins."

Darrell leaned closer to the holomap.

"Even with most of his forces out of the base, this is still going to be tough. We have to cover five miles undetected with enough equipment to bring down that building."

"True," Monica said.

"We don't need to take out the building," Moses said. "We need to take out the controllers."

The room was silent for a time. Darrell exhaled then slumped against to the couch.

"This is a suicide mission," he said.

Moses continued to look at the map. He was about to agree with Darrell until an idea came to his head.

"I have a way to get in," he said. "But we'll have to bring another player into the game."

"Another wild card, you mean," Monica commented.

"Maybe, maybe not," Moses replied. "Can I borrow a team?"

"No," Darrell blurted.

Miss Darla cut her eyes at him then looked at Moses.

"What do you need?"

- 8 -

The black Humvee rumbled up I-16, the persons inside nervous despite being well-armed and well trained. Moses sat in the passenger's seat upfront, gazing though the viewport. The driver occasionally glanced at him, a smile on her face. Moses took a quick look then smiled back.

"Never thought I'd see you again," Tanisha said.

"Why is that?" Moses asked.

"Cause you one of them wild-ass gunmen. I figured you'd be somewhere with another warlord or dead in a ditch."

"Sorry to disappoint you," Moses replied.

"Naw, naw, I'm good," Tanisha said. "I never got the chance to thank you properly after saving my ass."

"Your volunteering to take us to Fox Valley is thanks enough," Moses said.

"This ain't nothing." Tanisha stared at Moses then licked her lips. "I got plans."

Moses chuckled. "I don't think your mother would agree."

Tanisha scowled then turned her attention to the road.

"That woman still treats me like I'm five years old. Here I am driving a god-damn war truck kicking ass and taking names and when we get back she'll ask me did I eat."

"It's call concern," Moses said. "Cherish it while you have it. Once it's gone, you'll miss it forever."

"Now here you go getting all sentimental!" Tanisha shook her head.

Moses laughed. He looked ahead, searching for the turn off. Normally they would take the highway to the 96 exit, but that was too close to Jamal's territory. They would have to get off sooner and follow lesser roads to Fox Valley.

"Pull over here," Moses said.

Tanisha eased Bertha onto the dilapidated exit lane. Moses emerged slowly then crouched by the vehicle, his HK at his side. He scanned the area as best he could before sprinting to the road sign lying by the highway. He found what he was looking for. Moses sauntered back to the Humvee.

"Take this exit," Moses said. "It's the back way to Fox Valley."

Bertha revved the engine then steered Bertha up the rubble strewn exit.

"Is it safe?" she asked.

"I don't know," Moses replied, "but I'd rather take my chances this way than getting too close to Robbins."

The road was in terrible shape. They barely traveled five miles before they stopped for the night to set up camp. The night guard was set up and Moses took the first watch. Sitting alone at the edge of camp brought back memories he normally tried to avoid, but that night he let them come. He spent most of his life living just like this, roaming the

Wild, moving and hiding with his parents, avoiding any type of community except to trade or steal. He was surprised that he missed it sometimes. Living in Newlanta brought its own challenges. He was still struggling to get used to living among so many people. Crowds meant trouble as a young boy growing up; you can't keep your eye on everyone, his father used to say. Mama was less critical. She saw the goodness in everyone. It was her teaching that made him keep trying despite his survival instincts.

In the morning they broke camp and proceeded up the damaged thoroughfare. When they reached the first signs of the Fox Valley community Moses touched Tanisha's shoulder.

"Stop here," he said.

Tanisha steered Bertha into a cluster of pine trees.

"I'll walk from here," Moses said. "Don't want to drive up in this thing. We might find ourselves in a firefight."

"You ain't bulletproof," Tanisha said. "Besides, I'm not finished with you."

"You have a one-track mind," Moses said.

"Until I get what I want," Tanisha replied.

Moses opened the door.

"Good things come to those who wait," he said.

"It better be good, long as I've been waiting. Don't die."

"I won't."

Moses stepped out to the vehicle, checked his weapons then took his peace flag from his back pack. He attached the wire rod to the backpack, the white flag tied to the top. Slinging his guns to his side and back, he emerged from the thicket and made his way to the middle of the road. After about fifteen minutes of patient walking, he spotted the dust cloud of an approaching vehicle. As the jeep came into view, he raised his hands. The jeep continued to come, maintaining its speed. Moses became nervous; he lowered his hands a bit so they would be closer to his weapons. At the last minute the jeep swerved. The passengers jumped out with their guns trained on him.

"Down!" the closest man barked.

Moses eased onto his knees. The three guards walked up to him; one went behind him then pushed him down into the dirt with his foot.

"Hey!" Moses said. "Didn't you see my flag?"

"Fuck your flag," the man said. "We fell for that trick once."

The guards disarmed him then dragged him to the jeep. Moses hoped Tanisha and the others didn't see what was going on. They would come in guns blazing and screw everything up. As the jeep rumbled down the road, he kept his eyes on the horizon behind them. After a few more minutes he realized they were in the clear.

The jeep rumbled through Fox Valley to the city center. Things had changed drastically since his last visit. There were guards everywhere, even on the rooftops. The jeep took him to Shakira's office.

"Out," the guard ordered.

Moses complied. They marched him into the office. The receptionist looked up at Moses and frowned.

"Let the boss know we got another one," the man said.

The receptionist stood then knocked on Shakira's door. It opened moments later. Shakira's foul expression didn't change as she looked into Moses's eyes.

"Bring him inside," she said.

The guards took him inside the office.

"Get out," Shakira said.

The guards saluted. Shakira's expression changed from firm to shocked.

"What the fuck are you doing here?" she said. "Jamal's got everyone and their grandbabies looking for you!"

"Apparently they're not doing a good job," Moses replied. "I had to turn myself in to get caught."

"Cut the bullshit, Moses!" Shakira said. "This is serious!"

"I know, which is why I'm here."

Shakira shook her head as she pushed away from her desk.

"I don't want to hear it."

"You need to. Do you know what's about to happen?"

"God damn it Moses I told you I don't want to know!"

"Jamal has discovered war drones at Robbins and activated them. He wiped out the Knights and has his sights set on Newlanta."

Shakira's eyes, narrowed.

"I told you I didn't want to know."

"You don't get to sit this one out," Moses continued. "Once Jamal takes out Newlanta he's coming for you and everybody else."

"He has no reason to come for us," Shakira said. "We supply his food."

"Why buy the milk when you can own the cow?" Moses said.

Shakira slammed her fist on her desk.

"Fuck!"

She looked up at Moses.

"So, what do you want from me?"

"I have a team of Freedom Fighters waiting for me outside Fox Valley," Moses said. "We're going in to take out the drone command center. Without the drones we can stop Jamal."

"How do you plan to get inside?" Shakira asked.

"That's where you come in. We can get inside with your next shipment."

"Bullshit!" Shakira said. "I can't be a part of this!"

"You already are," Moses replied. "All of us are. Jamal can take the entire region with those drones. I've seen them in action, and you know I've been around. There's nothing that can stop those things except probably the Feds, and they have their own problems."

"I can't be involved," Shakira said. "If you fail I'm cooked."

"You haven't been listening," Moses said. "You and everyone else are going down regardless. You know Jamal better than I do. You know I'm right."

"Still though . . ."

"Okay, how about this. How about me and my team 'steal' a couple of your vehicles. We ambush them on their way to Robbins. We tie up the crew, take their credentials and use them to enter the base."

Shakira rubbed her chin. "That could happen."

"So you're in?"

Shakira nodded. "I'm going to have to lock you up for a few hours to make this all look legit. Jamal might have some eyes inside the town."

"I'm good with that," Moses said.

"There's a few folks I can put on that run that will know what's going to happen. I can trust them. You make sure they're not hurt."

"I will," Moses answered.

"Shit man, you always bring trouble."

"Not this time. I'm trying to prevent it."

Shakira stood.

"Good luck."

They shook then hugged.

Shakira took a moment to get her sour expression right before opening her office door.

"Take this man to a cell," she said.

"That won't be necessary," another woman said.

Moses stepped out the office and his eyes went wide. Shalonda Keys stood in the center of the office flanked by two of Jamal's soldiers.

"Jamal wants to speak with your guest," Keys said. "Don't worry, this won't reflect bad on you. I promise."

Shakira scanned the room before answering.

"Take him," she said. "He's your problem, not mine."

Jamal's men forced Moses' hands behind his back then cuffed him. Moses looked at Shakira; she mouthed the word 'sorry.' Moses shrugged.

Keys walked in front of them as they exited. A chopper waited in the city center.

"It seems I get the VIP treatment," Moses said.

"If it was up to me, I'd put a bullet in your head right here and be done with it," Keys said. "Just your luck Jamal likes to do his own wet work."

They were yards away from the chopper when it exploded. The blast shattered the windows of the town square buildings and knocked Moses and the others off their feet. Moses struck the ground on his side, then immediately rolled up to a sitting position in time to see Bertha bursting through the smoke followed by the Freedom Fighter team. Moments later Frack galloped through, heading toward him. The Humvee followed Frack to him then stopped; the Freedom Fighters jumped from the vehicles armed, armored and ready. The Fox Valley guards were moving in when Shakira's voice stopped them.

"Stand down, goddammit! Stand down!"

The Freedom Fighters drew on Shakira as she approached.

"No," Moses said. "She's on our side. She runs this show."

"You sure?" Tanisha said.

"I'm sure. Stand down."

Shakira walked up to them, shaking her head.

"You had this planned all along, didn't you?" Moses stood, glaring at Keys.

"No, she did." He looked at Tanisha. "And she did."

Tanisha walked over to Keys then pressed the barrel of her AR-15 against the woman's head.

"Keys, bitch."

Shalonda handed her the keys. Shakira pointed at the woman.

"Lock her up," she ordered.

Her men took Shalonda and the others away.

"I guess I can just give you the trucks now, seeing that I'm screwed," Shakira said.

Moses smiled. "The story stays the same, only now you can add that you were attacked. The Freedom Fighters will be just as fucked if this doesn't work."

"So, we're all depended on a crazy ass gunman."

Moses grinned. "Looks like it."

Shakira raised her hands. "Unbelievable."

Shakira's people took Shalonda and the others away to the jail. Tanisha swayed up to him, a mischievous smile on her face.

"Hey,' she said sweetly. "Good thing we showed up."

"You got lucky," Moses said.

"Not yet, but I'm counting on it."

Shakira joined them and Tanisha frowned.

"Tanisha, this is Shakira Lewis. She's mayor of Fox Valley."

The women shook hands.

"Good to meet you," Shakira said.

"Whatever," Tanisha replied.

"I appreciate your help, but I'm going to need you and your attitude out of my town ASAP," Shakira said.

Tanisha looked Shakira up and down before sucking her teeth then stomped back to the truck.

"You, too," Shakira said to Moses.

"We're gonna need those trucks," Moses reminded Shakira.

"You'll get the trucks," Shakira replied. "We'll meet at the ambush point."

"Thanks, Shakira."

"Yeah right. Now go."

Moses trailed Tanisha to Bertha, Frack close behind. Moses stopped to program Frack for stealth mode and the dog bot trotted away. He climbed into the vehicle.

"Which way?" Tanisha asked.

"The same way we came. We'll move to the main highway and wait for the food convoy once we get word from the second team. Any updates?

"Yeah. No major movement," Tanisha said.

"I hope they move soon. The longer they wait, the more likely they're going to hear about Shalonda's fiasco."

"They'll move when they move," Tanisha said "We can't do nothing about that."

They left the city taking a roundabout way to their ambush point. Moses hoped he would hear from the second team before dark, but that was not to be. That night he slept outside the Humvee again, laying on his back as he stared into the night sky. He heard the door close to Bertha and a grin came to his face. He sat up to see Tanisha strolling to him, a sly smile on her face. He sat up as she sat beside him.

"Finally!" she said.

"Don't you think we're a bit exposed . . ."

Tanisha pushed him on his back.

"Shut up," she said. She covered his mouth with hers, her tongue slipping between his lips as she pushed her hips against his crotch. Moses grabbed her ass with his hands and went with the moment.

* * *

"Damn!" Tanisha said. "That was good."

She rolled off Moses then put on her panties and pants. Moses lay still for a moment, letting his breathing settle. Tanisha stood then tucked her shirt in her pants.

"I feel like I owe you money."

Moses laughed as he pulled his underwear and pants from around his ankles. "I feel the same way."

Tanisha turned to walk away.

"Where you going?" Moses asked.

Tanisha looked over her shoulder. "Back to Bertha. Why?"

Moses sat up. "Why don't you come sit with me for a minute?"

Tanisha chuckled. "So, you one of them cuddling brothers."

"I wouldn't say that," Moses replied. "I just feel like it right now."

Tanisha walked back and sat beside him. "So what we gonna do? Talk?"

"That's a start," Moses replied.

Tanisha laid down on her side, resting her elbow on the ground to support her head. "What you want to talk about?"

"Nothing," Moses said. "I just want to sit here. With you."

"Aw shit now!" Tanisha said. She snuggled up against Moses. "You trying to make me your girlfriend or something?"

"Not really," Moses answered.

"Good, because I'm not available."

"Who's the lucky man?"

"Darrell."

Moses jumped up. "Darrell? Shit!"

Tanisha laughed. "Don't worry about it. That man don't own me. Besides, unless you tell him he won't know."

"There's a Humvee full of folks that might have something to say about that."

Tanisha shook her head. "They ain't gonna say nothing. That's my crew."

Tanisha laid down beside him.

"We out here fighting every damn day," she said. "We could be dead tomorrow. If Darrell ever gets around to asking me to marry him, or if I ask him, it's all good. Until then I'm living my life because I don't know when or where it might end. For real."

Moses nodded. He'd met people like Tanisha before, people living for the moment. It was easy to do in the Wild. He was the same way, but Newlanta changed his perspective. It was possible to live a long life in this world, to plan for the future, to think about family and long-term relationships. But in order for that to happen, there had to be someone willing to risk it all. People like him . . . and Tanisha.

"Well, congratulations to Darrell," Moses finally said.

"Don't congratulate him yet," Tanisha said. "You're pretty good. I feel a break up coming on."

They laughed as Moses put his arm around Tanisha and pulled her closer. They snuggled, looking into the night sky until they both fell asleep.

- 9 -

Moses woke to gentle nudging.

"Wake up, killer," Tanisha said. "We got a call from the ops team."

Moses rubbed his eyes as he sat up. Tanisha was up and walking to Bertha. The others were gathered around the Humvee. When Moses approach they all had smirks on their faces.

"Don't say a word," he said.

They laughed in response. Moses stuck his head in the Humvee; Tanisha sat in the driver's seat listening to the report.

"It's like a beehive around here," the ops team member said. "Not sure they're heading to Newlanta, but they're going somewhere."

"What about the drones?" Tanisha asked. "Seen them yet?"

"No," the ops leader replied. "Just conventional aircraft."

"Keep an eye out for them," Tanisha said. "They won't move on Newlanta without them."

Tanisha looked at Moses. "Well?"

"I'll contact Shakira. Looks like we're on."

Moses took out his comm and summoned Frack. Ten minutes later it trotted up to Bertha then sat beside him. He opened a comm to Shakira.

"Yeah," she said.

"We might get movement today."

"We'll get the trucks ready. One problem though."

"What's that?"

"Today is not a normal delivery day. It might draw suspicion."

"We'll deal with that when we get to it. Stand by."

"Got you."

The next few minutes were tense. They waited anxiously for word from the ops team, passing the time with card games and idle talk. Tanisha flirted with Moses, but he barely heard her. He was slipping into fight mode.

"Tanisha?"

Tanisha hit the comm. "Yeah. What's the word?".

"They're moving. We see the drones."

"Good. We're on our way."

Tanisha looked at Moses, her face serious.

"It's on," he said. He contacted Shakira.

"It's a go."

"The trucks are on the way," Shakira said. "I would wish you luck, but I know how you feel about that. Go get 'em, killer."

Moses switched the comm to Newlanta. The holo appeared above Frack's head.

"Speak," Voorhees said.

"They're on the way," Moses said. "I'm sorry."

"Don't apologize. It was inevitable. The good thing is that we know they're coming. Good luck Moses. We're in your hands."

Moses shut down the comm. He fought back the chill trying to take over his body. Never in his life had his actions determined the fate of so many people. He was tempted to walk away and disappear into the Wild. This was only his fight if he decided to stay. It would be a coward's move, except there was no such thing of cowards in the Wild. There was only the living and the dead, and in the Wild a person did anything and everything to live. He looked at Tanisha and the team preparing to risk their lives and he thought of Aisha and the others in Newlanta ready to die for what they'd built. In the end, it was the memory of his mother that kept him from walking away. This is what she dreamed of, a chance to build a world where people were safe, at least for a time.

"Okay," he thought. *"Let's do this."*

The supply trucks arrived 30 minutes later. The drivers and loaders exited then approached Moses and the patrollers. One of the drivers, an ebony hued man with a bald head and serious eyes approached Moses.

"You Moses?" he asked.

"Yep."

The man extended his hand and they shook.

"Johnny Jones," he said. "Shakira said you're the man running the show. Jamal's people know me and they'll be expecting me to be in the lead truck."

"You'll still be in the lead, but not in the truck," Moses said. "You'll ride with Tanisha in the Humvee."

Johnny rubbed his chin for a minute then nodded.

"Good, good. We don't normally come in protected but it will make sense based on what's been going on."

"The rest of us will load up in the food trucks. Where's the drop off?"

"We usually make the rounds," Johnny said. "There are a couple of commissaries on the base as well as a few small markets."

"Anything that takes you close to the center of the base?"

"The Officer's building," Johnny said. "There's a small commissary inside."

"Robbin's map," Moses said to Frack. A hol-omap floated between Moses and Johnny."

"Nice, nice," Johnny said.

"Show me the officers' building."

Johnny maneuvered around the map to get his bearings.

"Right here," he said as he pointed to a small building.

"Gather around," Moses called out. "The others circled Moses, Tanisha and Johnny. Moses searched the map for the building that housed the drone control team. When he found it, he pointed it out to the rest of the team.

"We won't be as close as I'd like to be, but we're close enough. We can make it work."

The map disappeared. Frack stood then trotted off.

"Let's do this then," Tanisha said.

Moses and the other patrollers loading into the supply trucks. Johnny boarded Bertha with Tanisha. They were on their way in minutes, speeding toward the base down Highway 96. Moses tapped his foot on the floor, distracting himself with a song his mother used to sing to him when they were alone. He glanced around the vehicle. The others looked back at him with nervous smiles. They were all aware that this might be a suicide mission, which went against everything Moses lived for. It was about survival; doing whatever had to be done to live another day. He shook his head to clear the thoughts. That was the Wildness in him. He had to think beyond himself, consider what he was doing in order save others.

The truck slowed. Moses's comm crackled with Tanisha's voice.

"First check point," she whispered.

"Let Johnny handle it," Moses said. "He knows what to do."

Moses gripped his HK and tilted the barrel toward the truck door. The others noticed his gesture and did the same. Five tense minutes passed before the truck began moving again.

"We're through the first gate," Tanisha said.

The truck jostled for another ten minutes before is stopped again.

"Hide your weapons" Tanisha shouted in his ear. Her voice was so loud the others heard her. When the truck gate slid up three troopers stood before them, guns drawn.

"Out," one of the men said.

Moses was the first to stand. He walked out of the truck, hands raised. The others followed.

"What's the problem?" Moses asked.

The trooper glared at him then entered the truck, the others following. As soon as they were in the truck Moses jumped in after them, his knife drawn. Two of the patrollers followed. He grabbed the last man in, slitting his throat before he could act. The other two spun around as the patrollers slammed into them, plunging their knives into their throats

Moses scrambled over the dying men, jumped out of the truck then sprinted to the Humvee. He snatched opened Johnny's door then motioned him out.

"Get in the truck," he ordered.

Johnny ran back to the truck. Moses sat beside Tanisha. As he was trapping in Frack came running from the distance. It halted beside the truck, the holo popping up immediately. Voorhees appeared, a distraught look on his face.

"They're here Moses, and it's not good. You got to take those drones out now!"

"We're on it!" Moses said. He slammed the door then stared at Tanisha.

"You know the way?"

"God damn right I do!"

"Hit it."

Tanisha hit the gas. Bertha's wheels spun, the vehicle pitching to the left for a minute before the tires took hold and they sprang forward. Tanisha's comm went live.

"What the fuck, Tanisha?" Johnny said.

"Newlanta's under attack," Moses answered. "No more time to be cute. We got to get to the drone building and take it out ASAP. Keep up as best as you can."

Tanisha sped down the narrow streets, handling Bertha like a car half its size. Moses sat ready on the guns, anticipating the moment they would be spotted. She kept to the side streets, which would take them longer but reduce their chances of being spotted before reaching the barracks.

"Tanisha! Johnny shouted.

"What?"

"Above you!"

Moses swiveled the gunsight to vertical. A chopper followed them, but wasn't descending.

"Company's coming," Moses said.

Moments later the armored cycles appeared in the rear-view mirror behind the food truck. Moses tapped his comm.

"Johnny, when the cycles reach you, stop."

"You want us to give up?"

"No, I want you to slow them down. Answer their questions; be polite. They'll think we're rogue. Once the fireworks start you can follow. Ditch the truck and come on foot."

"Gotcha."

Moses watched as the food truck did as told. Two of the cycles slowed with it; the other two continued to pursue Bertha.

"Look out your window," Tenisha said, her eyes still locked on the road. Two Humvees had joined the pursuit, keeping their distance but still following.

"You think they know where we're going?"

"I'm not sure," Moses answered. "Don't let them get ahead of us. I'm holding off making this a firefight as long as I can."

"You ain't got too much longer," Tanisha replied. "The barracks are straight ahead."

As the last words slipped through Tanisha's lips the pursuit closed in.

"We're blown!" Tanisha said.

She gunned the engine full throttle and Bertha lurched forward. Moses swung the guns forward, his targets the Humvees angling to block them. He presses the trigger and the Gatlings sprayed the vehicle to the left. The Humvee careened away, smashing into a building. The Humvee to the right veered away. Rounds smacked the top and rear of Bertha as the cycles and chopper fired at them. Moses ducked his head in reflex and Tanisha laughed.

"What? You scared? This ain't nothing. Bertha can handle this!"

Tanisha cut the wheel hard right. They were on the main road now, speeding directly for the barracks. Soldiers scrambled before them attempting to set up a barrier before the building. Moses aimed the Gatlings and fired. Soldiers fell and ran for cover, dropping the pylons meant to block their way. Two Humvees came from both sides of the building, both blocking the main entrance.

"It's going to get . . ."

The explosion rocked Bertha up onto two wheels. For a moment all Moses could do was pray as Tanisha fought to keep the vehicle from tipping over completely. When it slammed back onto four wheels Moses looked to the right and saw the tank.

"Holy shit!"

"Too little too late, motherfuckers!" Tanisha yelled. "We're going in!"

Moses didn't think Bertha had anything else in her, but she did. Tanisha shifted gears and the armored surged ahead toward the makeshift barrier. Moses braced for impact; Tanisha swerved to the right at the last minute.

"Shoot the fence!" she yelled.

Moses blasted the fence just before Bertha plowed through. There was nothing between them and the barracks, but Tanisha continued to speed.

"Tanisha?" Moses said.

"Hang on, baby!"

Bertha burst through the barracks entrance, barreling over the troops waiting behind the door to thwart them. The resistance of the walls and low ceiling slowed them but didn't stop them.

"Where's the room?" Tanisha said.

"On . . . on the bottom floor," Moses replied. "You're not going to drive down the stairs, are you?"

Tanisha laughed. "Hell naw!"

She slammed on the brakes at the top of the stairs.

"Come on, baby, it's you and me now."

Moses jumped from the vehicle with his HK. Tanisha stepped out with a Mossberg 12 gauge fitted with a barrel clip. She patted Bertha then kissed the door.

"Be right back, sugar."

It was a tight fit around Bertha to the stairs. Moses led the way down, his HK raised. When he reached the bottom of the stairs he peeked through the windows of the closed doors. More troopers waited. Moses took a grenade from his belt. Tanisha grabbed the door handles.

"Ready?" he said.

Tanisha nodded.

"Now!"

Tanisha jerked the door but it didn't budge.

"Fuck!" she shouted. She stepped back, fired three rounds into the lock mechanism then kicked the door. It flew open; the troopers guarding the drone control room responded with a hail of bullets. Moses managed to toss the grenade into the hallway before ducking for cover. The explosion rocked the hall; Moses was on his feet and running before the debris cleared, taking out those troopers that weren't killed by the blast.

Tanisha met him at the drone control room door. They peered through the window; the controllers looked back at them with wide eyes but continued their work. Moses yanked at the door. It was locked.

"Can't shoot through that," Tanisha said.

Moses smirked. "Yes, we can."

Tanisha's eyes lit up.

"Follow me!"

They sprinted down the hallway and up the stairs to Bertha. Tanisha took the toolbox from the back then climbed on top of the truck, detaching one of the Gatlings. She tossed it down to Moses. She climbed down then attached a handle to the gun.

"Get the ammo," she said.

Moses grabbed the ammo belts, wrapping what he could around his shoulders and dragging the rest behind him. They clambered down the stairs then back to the drone control room. Moses took the Gatling gun from Tanisha.

"Get into the stairwell just in case," he said.

Tanisha dashed for the stairwell. Moses braced himself then fired. The 20mm rounds ripped the door apart; Moses heard screams over the sound of the gun. He dropped the gun, switching to his HK. Tanisha jogged up to him, shotgun pressed into her hip.

"Get your asses out here now or we're coming in!" she shouted.

Some of the operators staggered into the hall bleeding; others came out with their hands raised.

"On the ground now!" Moses commanded. The controllers complied.

Moses ran into the room. The operators that had not come out the room lay dead. Moses moved through the room shutting down the consoles. He emerged into the hallway; Tanisha stood guard over the operators. He hit his comm.

"What's the situation out there?"

"We're in the building!" Johnny replied. "All hell is about to break loose. The base is under full alert. The Fighters arrived and attacked the southern section. They're drawing most of the fire, but units are coming for us. What's your status?

"The drone room has been neutralized."

"Well let's get the fuck out of here!"

Moses hesitated. "No. We hold the compound."

Tanisha's eyes bucked.

"What?"

"We hold the compound," Moses repeated. "This drone tech is too valuable to destroy."

Tanisha's eyes narrowed. "That wasn't the goddamn plan."

"Your army is here," Moses explained. "Jamal will be forced to break off his attack on Newlanta because without the drones he can't penetrate the walls. Voorhees will follow him back and attack to end the threat once and for all. All we need to do is hold out until it all comes together."

"If it comes together," Tanisha said.

"It will, trust me."

An explosion rocked the building. Tanisha ducked instinctively then glared at Moses.

"This is fucked up. You know that, right?"

"I got this," Moses said. "Keep an eye on them."

"What are you going to do?"

Moses looked at Tanisha and smiled.

"What I do best."

Moses slung the HK onto his back then grabbed the Gatling gun.

"Can I borrow Bertha?"

Tanisha shrugged. "Sure. Why not? It's not like I'm going to be living too much longer."

"I love your optimism. Be back in a few."

Moses climbed the stairs. When reached the top floor he saw the Fighters and the Fox Valley troops hunkered down. They had set up a makeshift barrier before the door. Moses hooked up the gun then climbed into the driver's seat. After a few tries he started Bertha. It took him a few minutes to turn it around, damaging more walls as he did so. Once he got it pointed toward the entrance, he opened the door.

"Get that shit out of the way!" he yelled.

The Fighters ran up to the door, dragging the barrier out of the way. Moses slammed on the gas and Bertha barreled down the hallway. Some of Jamal's soldiers got too anxious. They were rushing the cleared entrance when Moses burst out, running over them. Steering wheel in his left hand and joystick in his right, he swept the area with Gatling Gun fire as the Fighters replaced the barrier. He saw the tank in the distance trying to sight him, which is what he wanted. He drove an erratic pattern, scattering the attackers and making it difficult for the tank to target him. Once he's raised enough hell among the foot soldiers he sped away. The tank followed.

Moses had been in Jamal's base long enough to know where the ammo dump was located. It was his destination. An explosion to the right of Bertha shook him. He swerved for a moment then veered down a side road to put a few buildings between him and the tank. A Humvee appeared before him, the gunner opening fire. Sparks filled his view as .50 caliber rounds peppered Bertha, her shielding hold up to the lead onslaught. Moses answered with a sustained burst from the Gatling guns before taking a sharp left to avoid a head on collision. People scattered out of the way; Moses guided Bertha back to the main road and continued his run to the ammo dump.

An explosion lifted Bertha off her rear wheels. Moses held his breath as the vehicle lurched upward then fell back on the wheels. Moses saw a team of soldiers kneeling with shoulder rocket launchers; he swung the Gatlings to the rear and cut them down.

The ammo dump appeared, only a few yards away. As he neared, he saw the tank barreling after him. Moses slowed as if he didn't see it, hoping his timing would be perfect.

"One . . . two . . . now!"

Moses jerked the wheel right as the tank fired. The shell whizzed by so close he heard it, then smiled as it hit the ammo dump. The initial explosion rocked Bertha; the second explosion spun the armored truck around like a child's toy, Moses hanging onto the steering wheel hoping Bertha would go into a roll. She didn't. As soon as the truck stopped spinning Moses sped away. He parked the truck behind a building a few blocks away, checked his weapons then climbed out. He hated leaving it behind, but he had work to do and the truck was too big of a target, especially with a tank and who knew what else hunting for it. He peeked from behind the building. The tank was cruising toward the wrecked and burning building. Fire crews arrived as well, hoping to douse the flames before more ammo exploded. They were too late. People scattered as the rounds went off, sending stray bullets flying in every direction. Moses grinned then ran back to the drone compound. Moses made his way back he spotted more of Jamal's troops running in the direction of the drone barracks. Whatever troops remaining in Jamal's compound had the building surrounded. Moses crouched behind a wall, watching the troops move into position as he took his .308 from his back. It took him only a few minutes to find a good perch. He hit his comm.

"Tanisha."

"Moses? Where the fuck are you?"

"I'm near the drone barracks. Jamal's troops have you surrounded. I'm about to lay sniper fire. I'll pin them down and y'all can get the hell out of that trap. Once you're out you know where to go."

"I thought we were holding the building."

"It's too hot. You got to get out now."

"Where's my truck?"

"It's safe."

"If you damaged Bertha I'm gonna . . ."

"Tanisha, stay focused! Count to five then head for the entrance."

Moses shut off the comm then took aim. He took out five troopers before they realized they were under fire from the rear. The troopers scrambled for cover. A few tried to work their way toward him. That was a mistake. They lay face first on the ground, .308 rounds in their foreheads. Moses swung his scope to the drone building entrance; the Freedom Fighters hurried out, taking their captives with them. Moses swung the sniper rifle onto his back then signaled Frack. He grabbed his HK and moved in.

Frack ran by him as he approached the troopers, creating the diversion he needed. The hidden soldiers fired at it in response, revealing their positions. Moses worked his way closer then encountered a cluster of troopers massing to charge the building He opened fire, taking down three before the rest could find cover. He was moving before they could return fire, working his way toward the building. A trooper surprised him; he jumped for cover, bullets flying over his body, one creasing his back. Moses stayed low, listening to the trooper running toward him. He opened fire as the man's legs came into view then fired a few more rounds into him as he fell to the round. He rolled into a squat, grimacing from the wound on his back. But he couldn't stay still. He worked his way to the rear of the building, following the Freedom Fighters in hopes of linking up with them. Gunfire erupted around him and once again he was scrambling for cover. The troopers were coming from both sides, having worked their way around the building before he could. He was pinned down.

More gunfire erupted and the troopers scattered. Moses dared to look up from cover and smiled in relief. Shakira ran toward him, followed by twenty Wildcats.

"Shakira!" he shouted.

Shakira raised her AR-15, a puzzled look on her face.

"Moses?"

Moses emerged from hiding and Shakira grinned.

"What the hell are you doing here?" he said.

"I'm already fucked, so I figured we might as well try to get something out of this shit," she replied.

The Wildcats battled the troopers, both groups holding their positions.

"What's the situation?" Shakira asked.

"We got the drone station," Moses said. "We captured the controls and took them with us."

"He's gonna be pissed," Shakira said. "So much for my good thing."

"I don't know," Moses said. "Freedom Fighters are here in full force. They're holding the southside of the base. Having you here helps."

"I have one hundred people," Shakira said. "That's not much. When Jamal gets back, we'll be overwhelmed."

"I think Jamal has his own problems right now," Moses said.

A bullet struck the wall above them and they ducked in reflex.

"Voorhees is not sitting on his ass. I'm sure as soon as those drones went down, he counterattacked."

"How good are his forces?"

"Good enough," Moses answered. "They have passion on their side. Jamal is fighting for greed. Voorhees is fighting for love. That makes a difference."

"So, what do we do?" Shakira asked. The smirk on her face told she already knew the answer. Moses smirked back.

"We take this damn base, killer," he said.

Moses touched his comm.

"Tanisha?"

"What?"

"Secure the prisoners then get y'all asses back up here. We're about to take this bitch."

"I just want my Bertha back!"

"You'll get that and some."

An explosion rocked their position.

"That fucking tank!" Moses shouted.

Shakira grinned.

"We got something for that."

The Wildcats were already responding. Three fighters with rocket launchers had moved into position.

"Hit it!" Shakira yelled.

Moses, Shakira and the other Wildcats laid down cover fire. The rocket men jumped up, took aim and fired. Each rocket found it its mark, destroying the tank.

"Let's move!" Moses shouted.

The Wildcats jumped into action, Moses and Shakira leading the way. They worked as a team like they did years past, alternating between advance and cover, clearing the streets and buildings with precision. It helped that Jamal had taken his veteran fighters with him for the assault on Newlanta; those left behind had little fighting experience. The Freedom Fighters joined them soon afterwards, supported by their armored trucks. The Robbins defense faltered in minutes, the troopers running in every direction with the civilians caught in the crossfire. Soon Moses and Shakira were walking in the open unopposed.

They were sweeping the main road when Tanisha drove up with Bertha. She jumped out the vehicle with a grin on her face.

"Looks like we won this one," she said.

"It's not over yet," Moses said. He took out his homing comm and pressed it. Ten minutes later Frack trotted up to them. It was damaged but still mobile. He touched the head unit for the holo link to Newlanta. Seconds later Voorhees image appeared. He was seating in a vehicle, bouncing as it sped.

"Voorhees, it's Moses. What's your status?"

"We're pursuing Jamal down I75," Voorhees said. "His foot soldiers have either scattered or surrendered. What's your status?"

"The base is ours," Moses said.

"Excellent! We'll be there soon."

"We're sending a team up the highway," Moses said. "We can catch him between us."

"That's not necessary," Voorhees replied. "If we have the base, Jamal is finished."

"You don't know him like I do," Moses said. "Jamal will be a thorn in your side as long as he's alive."

"So, you're finally going to do what we sent you to do?"

Moses laughed. "Sometimes you have to take the long way to get where you're going."

Moses shut off the comm.

"Come on Tanisha," he said. "Let's go kill a rat."

Moses hopped into Bertha. Tanisha hit her comm.

"Patrollers! Follow me!"

The Freedom Fighter convoy sped down the main road to I-75. Once they reached the highway they spread out, taking up the north and southbound lanes. Rouge bands appeared on the highway perimeter taking potshots at the convoy but were easily dispersed by a few rounds from the Gatlings. Moses kept his eyes forward, looking for signs of Jamal's convoy. They sped through Macon without incident, threading through damaged stretches of highway. They picked up the pace once through the dilapidated city. As they reached Forsyth, Moses's comm buzzed.

"Who is this?" he asked.

"Voorhees. Jamal's group had decided to make a stand in Forsyth."

Moses nodded. "We're almost there. What's your location?"

"Northside of the city, near the abandoned retail district."

"I know it well," Moses said. "Tricky area. We'll have to go in on foot. Pull your soldiers back and form a perimeter."

"We can handle this," Voorhees said.

"No, you can't," Moses replied. "This is wet work. Pull'em back and hold the highway."

Voorhees cut the comm.

"We going in?" Tanisha asked.

"No," Moses replied. "I know this area well. Form a barrier on the outside. I'll go in and flush them out."

"I'll go too," Tanisha said.

"No. I need you out here with Bertha just in case they try to break out and head south."

"So, you're really going in by yourself?"

Moses nodded.

Tanisha leaned over and kissed his cheek.

"I love your crazy ass!"

Moses laughed despite himself.

"Let's hope there's some of my crazy ass left to love when this is over."

The Freedom Fighter vehicles pulled off the highway before the Forsyth retail district. They spread out, keeping enough distance between them to make it difficult to take them out all at once. Moses checked his HK, and Sig Saur. He unclipped his machete then put on his goggles.

"Remember, no one else comes in," Moses said. "If I see you, I'm shooting you."

He turned and winked at Tanisha.

"Cover me."

Moses jumped out of Bertha then sprinted for the nearest cover. He jumped from hiding spot to hiding spot, but he was sure there would be no fire. Jamal knew better that to expose is position. In the open he would lose, but in the wreckage of the retail area he was at an advantage. He knew the ruins almost as well as Moses did.

Moses lay on his belly and crawled into the first building, gripping his HK. He reached the first door then peeked around the corner. The scrap of a boot against the floor was his only warning; he rolled onto his back, blocking the machete strike with his gun. He rolled right, kicking his attacker away with a boot to the ribs. Moses then let go of his gun then rolled on top of the man, punching him in the mouth while holding down his right hand which held the machete. His second blow was to the man's throat. The man gasped and his grip loosened. Moses held him down until he stilled.

Moses grabbed his machete then snatched his free from his back. The building echoed with boots striking the ground. Moses crouched, machete in each hand as other fighters ran toward him, their blades drawn. Five men surrounded him, each apparently skilled knife fighters. Moses had no time to waste.

He feinted at the two in front of him, drawing the three behind him to attack. Moses stepped to his left, crossing the machetes to block a thrust from the closest man the slashing his throat with the machete in his right hand. He ducked a swing then stabbed the man in his foot as he attacked the third man, kicking his shin then stabbing him in the stomach. He flinched as another man managed to slash his thigh. He returned the favor by cutting the man's hand off. The last fighter standing charged him and they dueled. One machete was no match for Moses wielding two. He cut and stabbed the man to his knees.

More troopers were running his way. Moses dropped the dead man's machete then shoved his machete back into his sheath. He picked up his HK. Jamal's men were using blades in order to keep their positions secret; at this point there were too many for Moses to so the same. He spun around as he unloaded the HK, taking the men down. They would know where he was, at least for the moment. Moses ran along the edge of the open warehouse, hoping to find another place to hide before the bulk of Jamal's team reached the building. He was ducking into a doorway then the shots rang out. His comm buzzed.

"Moses! You okay?" Tanisha asked.

"No," he replied.

"Dammit we're coming in!"

"Stay the fuck out!" he said. "Jamal and his crew know this building. They'll cut you apart."

Moses ducked into a small hole that led to the basement. He dropped to the floor in a crouch then found a hiding place among a pile of rotted furniture.

"This is going to take while," he said. "A long while. Be patient and watch the doors. Shoot anybody that comes out."

"We should just bomb the shit of this bitch and be done with it," Tanisha said.

"Won't work," Moses replied. "Like I said, be patient and let me do my job."

Moses took his comm out of his ear and shoved it into his pocket. He sat in his hiding place and closed his eyes, bringing up a metal map of the building and figuring out a plan to work every inch of it.

"Okay killer. Let's get it done."

For the next hour Moses worked with lethal efficiency, taking out Jamal's men in groups of ones and twos. He had no idea how many had escaped into the building, but the occasional outburst of gunfire told him that a few had opted to make a run for it rather than deal with him. He scoured the building twice, coming across bodies of those he'd already dispatched. Still, no Jamal. It was possible he fled and was gunned downed outside. Moses decided to do one more sweep then leave the killing grounds.

He was entering the old restaurant section when he heard the footfall behind him. As he spun around, he saw Jamal running at him, his machete aimed for Moses's mid-section. Moses twisted to his right and Jamal adjusted his blade, slicing Moses stomach. Moses yanked his machete free then swung at Jamal's neck but the man ducked and Moses cut air. He turned to face Jamal, blood soaking his shirt.

"Motherfucker," Jamal said.

He attacked again. Moses met him head on and the two dueled across the littered floor, the sound of their machetes clashing filling the empty space. The last thing Moses wanted was a knife fight with Jamal. The man was good with machetes, too good. Although he kept Jamal from landing a killing blow, the small slashes and cuts were slowly taking their toll. Moses struggled to stay on his feet while Jamal seemed to be inexhaustible.

"You had to come back and fuck things up," Jamal said. "I should have killed you a long time ago."

Moses managed to smile. "Yet here we are."

Jamal ran at him again. Moses blocked another stab at his throat then winced as Jamal stomped his foot. He knew it was a distraction but he couldn't stop his arm from reaching down. Jamal's machete sank into his stomach as a shot rang out. As Moses fell backwards, he saw Jamal stand rigid, his eyes glassing over as he fell to his knees then face forward. Moses hit the ground hard, his eyesight blurring. Tanisha appeared over him, her eyes glistening.

"Oh no! Oh no!"

Moses managed to smile.

"I told you to stay outside," he said.

Tanisha's lips moved but he couldn't hear her. Her face faded, then the world turned dark.

- 1 0 -

Moses opened his eyes to muted light. As he shifted, he remembered why he was prone, so he eased his head left to right. He lay in bed in a sparse room, a metal desk near his head, the surface covered with small containers and a pitcher of water. He was about to sit when a voice interrupted him.

"You don't want to do that," the woman said.

Moses grimaced as he turned to his side. The woman standing beside the bed wore a lab coat and held a clip pad. She shared a warm smile with him.

"I'm Dr. Haddish," she said.

"Moses Pritchard," he replied.

"Well Mr. Pritchard, you took a pretty bad cut there. Didn't know if we were going to be able to save you."

Moses nodded. "Thanks for being honest."

"It's easy when you save someone."

Dr. Haddish checked his vitals.

"Where am I?" Moses asked.

"Robbins medical compound," the doctor replied. "You were too bad off to take to Newlanta so we treated you here."

"I'm surprised, in light of what happened."

Dr. Haddish shrugged. "I'm a doctor. I treat the sick and injured. I don't take sides. Besides, this might be the best thing that ever happened to us."

"You think so?" Moses asked.

"Um hmm. Newlanta medics brought us some amazing equipment. I didn't know such things existed. They've also been very gracious with everyone, even the soldiers."

Moses grinned. "I see you've met the Retrievers."

"That's what they call them? Whoever they are, they're wonderful."

Voorhees wasn't wasting anytime assimilating Robbins. It was probably his plan all along.

Someone knocked on the door.

"Come in," Dr. Haddish said.

The door swung open and Shakira stepped inside with a smirk on her face.

"I'll be damned. You did survive. I lost that bet."

Moses chuckled. Dr. Haddish was not amused.

"I'm going to have to ask you to leave," she said.

"It's alright, doc," Moses said. "Shakira's a friend. Can you give us a few minutes?"

The doctor glared at Shakira as she left the room. Shakira pulled up the metal chair, turning it backwards before sitting down and propping her arms on the backrest.

"You look like shit," she said.

"I bet I look better than Jamal. Nice shot, by the way."

"It felt as good as it looked. I hated that bastard."

Moses laughed and it hurt. "So, what's the situation?"

Shakira reached into her pocket and took out a toothpick. She stuck it between her teeth.

"Me, Voorhees and The Freedom Fighters are having a pow wow on how to share the spoils."

Moses's eyebrows rose. "Share? Interesting."

"Ain't it, though," Shakira replied. "Especially since Voorhees has the upper hand. It was his idea."

"Sounds like him," Moses said.

"How long you got here?" Shakira asked.

"You'll have to ask the doctor you pissed off."

"Shit, I don't want to know that bad."

Shakira stood then winked.

"Get better, killer."

Moses saluted. "Yep."

Shakira sauntered out the room. Two minutes later Dr. Haddish returned.

"That was unpleasant," she said.

Moses chuckled. "Shakira is good people. She just a little blunt."

"A little?" Dr. Haddish rolled her eyes.

"Anyway, you've got at least another week in this bed. Once you're healed up enough will transfer you to Newlanta."

"Thank you, doc."

"No, thank you, Mr. Pritchard. From what I hear we owe you a lot."

"Nobody owes anyone anything," Moses replied. "And call me Moses."

"Get some rest, Moses." The doctor smiled then left the room.

Moses leaned back on his pillow and fell immediately to sleep. He couldn't remember the last time he was able to rest like this. It figured it had to be a wound to make it happen. He was always moving from one tense situation to another, always restless like his father. When he finally woke again, it was dark. The kerosene lamp on his nightstand had been lit, and there was a fresh pitcher of water there as well.

"Moses?"

Moses grinned as he recognized the familiar soothing voice. He sat up then rubbed his eyes. It still hurt to move, but not as much as it did the day before. Turning his head to the direction of the voice, he nodded at Miss Darla. She sat in the only seat in the room, flanked by Monica and Darrell.

"It's good to see you're healing," Miss Darla said.

"It's good to be seen," Moses replied.

Miss Darla laughed. "All these old saying coming out of your young mouth. You have an old soul, Moses Pritchard."

Moses shifted about, trying to get more comfortable.

"Be careful," Miss Darla said. "You don't want to tear nothing." She glanced at Monica. Her daughter nodded then ambled to the table. She put a canvas bag on it. Monica shared a quick smile then returned to her mother's side.

"A few things from the farm," Miss Darla said. "They'll help get you right and speed your healing. I put a list of instructions inside.

"Between you and Dr. Haddish I should be climbing trees in no time."

"I don't know about all that," Miss Darla said.

"I suspect you came up for the meeting?" Moses asked.

"That, too. But I really wanted to come up to thank you for what you did, Moses. You could have as soon served us up to Jamal than help us. It wouldn't have made no difference in your plan, yet you chose to help us."

"It was the right thing to do," Moses said.

"Help me up, children," Miss Darla said.

Monica and Darrell gently lifted Miss Darla to her feet. They followed her as she walked to the door.

"Your mother is proud of you," she said. "This is what she wants you to do."

"You talk like she's still here," Moses said.

"She is." Miss Darla looked up. "They are. They all are. They're watching us, and we've got to do right by them."

Moses was puzzled. "Who is watching us?"

Miss Darla looked at Moses with a gleam in her eyes.

"The ancestors. When you're healed up, come on down to visit. We have a lot to talk about."

Miss Darla and her family left the room. Moses stared at where they once stood, his mind a mix of emotions. Miss Darla mentioning his mother brought sadness and joy. This was what she wanted him to do; he was sorry she wasn't still here to see it. Yet in Miss Darla's mind, she was. Moses looked up as tears formed in his eyes.

"Mama, Papa; I hope you can see this," he said. "I hope it's okay."

He lay back down and closed his eyes, thankful for Miss Darla's visit.

* * *

The morning of the third day brought Moses back to reality. Dr. Haddish entered his room with the morning meal and two visitors; Voorhees and Esmerelda.

"Good morning, Mr. Pritchard!" the doctor said.

Moses sat up with a smirk.

"It was until y'all entered. Looks like I'm back on the clock."

"Looks like it," Esmerelda said. "Hey, where are my dogs."

Moses raised his hands. "Does it look like I'm interested where they are?"

Dr. Haddish examined him while Voorhees and Esmerelda sat.

"You're recovering well," she said. Her smile faded when she spotted the bag from Miss Darla.

"What's this?" she asked.

"Some root medicine from the Freedom Fighters," Moses replied.

Dr. Haddish went to the table, grabbed the bag and opened it. Her nose crinkled like she was inspecting the garbage.

"You don't believe in root medicine?" Moses asked.

"Root medicine has its merits," the doctor said. "What I don't believe in is conflicting treatments. I'll check this out to make sure it works."

She shifted her attention to Voorhees and Esmerelda.

"Don't be too long. This man needs rest."

The doctor left the room. Esmerelda immediately began rifling through his clothes.

"Excuse me?" Moses said.

"I'm looking for your call comm," she said. "I need to check out the dogs."

Moses reached to the table, grabbed the comm then tossed it to her.

"Last I saw Frack was fine," he said. "I lost Frick in Forsyth weeks ago."

"Check," Esmerelda said. "Frick has a GPS. We should be able to find it unless it's been scavenged. I'll leave you two to your conversation."

Moses watched her leave the room.

"And I thought she was worried about me," he commented.

"We all were," Voorhees said.

"Congratulations on your victory," Moses said. "Robbins is yours."

"The congratulations go to you," Voorhees replied. "This wouldn't have happened without your plan."

Moses laughed. "Plan? Yeah, right. This shit came together on its own. I was just supposed to kill a man, remember?"

"Sometimes the best plans are spontaneous," Voorhees said. "It's the sign of a great leader."

Moses's eyes narrowed. "You're not about to start that again, are you?"

"Because of you we have a peaceful corridor running the entire length of old I-75. In addition, we have access to the tech Jamal discovered at Robbins. This is the greatest thing to happen to this region since the Collapse."

"So, what are you going to do with it, Voorhees? Who's running the show? Are you the baddest warlord in the land now?"

Voorhees frowned. "You know I don't think that way. All I want is peace. With what has happened we have a good chance of securing that. Shakira, Miss Darla and I have made great progress in combining our communities. There's also talks of bringing the Knights into the discussion as well."

"Now you've lost me," Moses said. "Some groups can't be changed."

"We'll see," Voorhees said. "Everyone deserves a chance."

"And if it doesn't work out?"

Voorhees smiled. "Then we have you."

Moses laughed. "A gunman's peace."

Voorhees looked puzzled. "What?"

"A gunman's peace. That's what my daddy called it," Moses said. "He used to say that the only way to keep the bad guys away was to be badder than them. If you have a gun, you'll have peace."

"That's a sad way to look at it," Voorhees said.

"Yet here we are," Moses replied.

The two were silent for a moment.

"Moses, I'm going to say this, and I hope you don't take it personally," Voorhees said. "I wish people like you didn't have to exist."

Moses smirked. "I do, too. You think I enjoy this? Now there are some gunmen out there that thrive on violence. I've met a few, and I've killed a lot. But me, no. It's a necessity. If I had it my way, I'd never have picked up a gun. If I could toss them today I would. That's what I was trying to do in Newlanta until y'all found me."

"I guess I should apologize for that," Voorhees said.

"No need to. You needed protection. I could have turned you down, but I didn't."

"Why?"

"Because my mama wouldn't have wanted me to," Moses said. "When me and my daddy lost her, we lost our souls. That's when we took on mercenary work. Daddy didn't care about people anymore, and neither did I. He died with that anger, and I almost did."

Voorhees stood. "You're a good man, Moses. Don't let anyone tell you different."

Moses nodded, although inside he didn't believe Voorhees's words.

"When you get better come see me. We've got work to do."

Voorhees left the room. Moses let his head fall onto his pillow. He stared into the cracked ceiling. He was lucky. He should have died, but he didn't. So many others weren't so fortunate. When did it all end? Would the world his mother dreamed of ever be? Moses laughed; of course it wouldn't. The one thing he'd learned over the years is that people will find reasons to kill each other no matter what their circumstances. The best anyone could do is keep it contained. Voorhees believed different. Miss Darla did, too.

It took almost two months of healing for Moses to be able to travel. Dr. Haddish insisted that he take a few more weeks of rest, but Moses was done with laying around. He acquired a decent motorbike from the Robbins mechanic shop then headed south to Freedomland. He spent the winter there, connecting with the local folks and learning about the ancestors from Miss Darla. He also spent a lot of time with Tanisha, against her mother's best wishes. Most surprising of all, he saw the Knights work with the Freedom Folk. The Knights didn't have a choice; Jamal's attack devastated their farms and killed most of their fighters. It's funny how desperation cools hate, he thought. Hopefully their transformation wouldn't be temporary. If it was, he knew the Fighters could handle themselves until help from Newlanta arrived.

In the spring he traveled to Fox Valley. He spent two months with Shakira, helping her train

her police force and overseeing the transfer of Newlanta tech to the small city. By the time he departed
the city had working electricity to all the household
and the foundation of a local net. Future plans were
to connect with Newlanta, but that would take some
time. Despite her best efforts Esmerelda had yet to
find an active satellite. Some Old-World tech continued to remain hidden.

Moses returned to Newlanta during the fall.
The oaks and other hardwoods were changing colors, adding autumn brilliance to the otherwise
bland cityscape. The ride up I75 had been unevent-
ful, an indication that the alliance was holding and
being enforced. Moses had been gone so long it took
him longer than expected to enter the city. It came
down to a call directly from Voorhees's office for
him to gain access. Voorhees requested that he report immediately, but Moses had other plans. He
stopped at the Buckhead market, picking up a bun-
dle of late season flowers and hard candy before
riding to the high rise. He caught the newly reno-
vated elevator to Zenobia's floor then sauntered
down the hallway to her apartment. Moses was
nervous as he knocked on the door; he'd been gone
so long it was possible she'd moved on. He couldn't
blame her; it wasn't like he'd been celibate during
their time apart. The door opened and Moses found
himself staring at a woman he didn't recognize.

"Yes?"

Moses smiled as he hid his disappointment.
"Sorry, I have the wrong apartment."

"It happens," the woman said. She was about
to close the door then hesitated.

"Are you looking for Zenobia?"

Moses's face lit up. "Yes, I am!"

The woman smiled. "Wait just a minute."

She walked away then returned with an envelope.

"She told me to give this to you if you ever returned."

"Thank you," Moses said.

"No problem," the woman said. "Have better one."

Moses waited until he was back downstairs on his bike before opening the envelope. What he read made him smile.

Hey you! Where have you been? If you're reading this, you know I'm gone. I decided to move outside of the Perimeter. You were right about Carmen. I kicked her ass out. I'm living at the communal farm towers in Alpharetta. Things have settled down in the Wild, and the word is you had something to do with it. If you're planning on sticking around, come see me. Did I wait for you? There's only one way to find out.

Love,
Zee

Moses folded the note and stuffed it in his pocket. He took out his comm then contacted Voorhees.

"Moses?"

"In the flesh."

"Where are you?"

"I'm in Newlanta."

"Excellent. We'll meet this afternoon."

"Let's make that tomorrow. I have one more stop to make."

"Moses, you don't realize how important it is . . ."

"I do, Voorhees. But this is more important. How do I get to the Alpharetta farms?"

Voorhees sighed. "Exit the North Gate and take 75. You can't miss it."

"Thanks. See you tomorrow?"

"Maybe."

Moses shut off the comm. He and Voorhees had plenty of time ahead to talk, but for now, Moses had to attend to something more important. He started the bike and headed for the North Gate.

-End-

ABOUT THE AUTHOR

Milton J. Davis is an award winning Black Speculative fiction writer and owner of MVmedia, LLC, a small publishing company specializing in Science Fiction, Fantasy and Sword and Soul. Milton is the author of nineteen novels and editor/co-editor of seven anthologies. Milton's work had been featured in *Black Power: The Superhero Anthology*; Skelos 2: *The Journal of Weird Fiction and Dark Fantasy Volume 2, Steampunk Writers Around the World* published by Luna Press and *Bass Reeves Frontier Marshal Volume Two*. Milton's story 'The Swarm' was nominated for the 2018 British Science Fiction Association Award for Short Fiction.

For more action-packed adventure by Milton J. Davis and other authors, visit www.mvmediaatl.com, The Best of the Black Fantastic.

CPSIA information can be obtained
at www.ICGtesting.com
Printed in the USA
LVHW032257110720
660354LV00005B/314

9 780999 278987